MW01232188

HATE TO LOVE YOU

SHORT STORY COLLECTION

SABRINA B. SCALES   KELSEY GREEN

CANDICE JOHNSON   KIMMIE FERRELL

Rose Gold Press, LLC
Chicago, Illinois
www.RoseGoldPress.com

Paperback ISBN: 978-1-7354167-2-4

Editor:
Nicole Falls
Trim and Polish

Cover Design:
Sherelle Green

HATE TO LOVE YOU

SHORT STORY COLLECTION

There's a thin line between love and hate... Or is it?

Rose Gold Press is excited to bring you a collection of four short, page-turning love stories. From sweet and heart-warming moments to hot and steamy love scenes, the unforgettable characters in this collection are bringing you a little sweet, dipped in a whole lot of sexy.

The Art of Love by **Kelsey Green**

All it took was one night to bring Peyton back into Hasani's life. But with passion, lust and revelations seeping from every blurry memory, Hasani will have to do her best to remember how it all fits together. For the art of love is painted in the details.

Stuck With You by **Kimmie Ferrell**

Landon only has ten days to show Gianna he's not the

man she thinks he is. But the uphill battle to win her heart is not easy. As the two rival event planners work to pull off the wedding of the century, they realize sometimes the best kind of love is unplanned.

Uber Intentions **by Candice Johnson**

Laken's debut novel is poised to blow up every book list. But author Knight's poisonous pen - and plagiarism lawsuit - threatens her potential best-selling title. Not only are they former secret friends with benefits, but they're essentially telling the same story. Will Knight and Laken remain enemies? Or will they reconcile… via Uber?

Restored **by Sabrina B. Scales**

Ten years after their bad break-up, Deja and Orlando are forced to spend time together. As expected, tensions are high and it's impossible to imagine reconciliation after such a long rift. Will Lando and Deja be able to restore what was lost or will they continue down two paths leading in opposite directions?

THE ART OF LOVE

KELSEY GREEN

All it took was one night to bring Peyton back into Hasani's life. But with passion, lust and revelations seeping from every blurry memory, Hasani will have to do her best to remember how it all fits together. For the art of love is painted in the details.

To Kenny, you are the Pierre to my Hasani and life wouldn't be as crazy without you.

CHAPTER ONE

Hasani

Fuck. My. Life.

My head was pounding as I slowly forced my eyes open trying to ignore the shooting pain resulting from every micromovement my muscles made. The room was drowned in morning sunlight that streamed in from every nook and cranny. Despite the high irritation the brightness caused my aggressive hangover, I found it soothing for once, since it meant despite my spotty memory of last night, I had ended up somewhere safe. No better confirmation than knowing that regardless of how wild and reckless my night may had gotten, at some point, a clearer mind had prevailed and landed me in my best friend Pierre's luxurious two-bedroom condo in the end.

The window dressings in the guest bedroom were sheer because in Pierre's world – *design chooses you. You do NOT choose the design*. In other words, the extremely fluffy, contemporary bedroom would forever have see-through curtains because the room had chosen them for itself. No one could convince Pierre that darker, blackout curtains were an option, since it was *not his choice* at all. His logic made no damn sense, but I'd learned early in life that interior design was one of those topics that was useless to debate him on.

As I slowly sat up, I reached out for the glass of water Pierre always left on the nightstand whenever I stayed over, but surprisingly found it empty. Clearly, he was slipping on his best friend duties. Glancing at the rest of the bed before allowing my heavy eyelids to fall once more, I observed the tussled half removed sheets, implying I'd returned to my sporadic sleeping habits. As a kid, I'd always tossed and turned a lot, causing my parents to get me adapted to sleeping in my own bed at an early age. And now that I was an adult and had a bit more control of my body, I usually slept a lot more calmly. Except, apparently, when I'd had a stressful day that took over my dream state as well.

Letting out a quick sigh, I continued my attempt at standing, sliding gently off the bed. However, the minute my toes lightly grazed something soft and taut, I completely lost my balance, ungracefully descending to the ground, taking the remaining sheets with me.

"Ugh."

I froze. *Okay that deep voice sure as hell wasn't me and definitely didn't belong to Pierre*, my thoughts screeched as panic raced through my mind. Given my pounding headache, I hoped and almost convinced myself that the husky grunt I'd heard upon falling to the floor belonged to my own higher pitched voice. But unfortunately, the realization that I'd landed on top of another person and not the ground was all too apparent in the milliseconds that followed.

"So first you kick me out the bed and then you pounce on me?"

I was too shocked to respond, but his heavy voice was all too familiar, even with the slight gravelly tone. He remained unmoving beneath me for what felt like an hour, but in reality, was only a few seconds. Long enough for me to feel his hands grazing my hips, feel his groin planted perfectly between my legs and feel my heartbeat quicken to the same pace as his.

I was as naked as a turkey on Thanksgiving morning and I had no memory of how I'd ended up that way. And just in case that wasn't enough of a reason to freak out, it appeared that despite the sheet landing around me, all of my goodies were on full display.

The next insight that came flooding in through the surge of fear was the understanding that my bed partner —*now floor partner*—was none other than Peyton Stone, a man that I'd known as long as I'd known Pierre. A man I'd met when we were both just stupid kids. A man who until this very moment—or apparently last night—had never seen me naked. *A line we'd never be able to uncross.*

As every thought rushed through my head at once, I clung to the most obvious one first. Needing to calm my mind before the pain from my headache and spiral of emotions caused me to pass out altogether, I asked, "What are you doing here, Stone?"

"Sleeping before you plowed back on top of me," he replied.

"No, I mean what are you doing in Miami? In Pierre's condo?" I slowly began pushing off his chest that was still covered by the blanket he'd had over him before his words registered.

"Wait, did you say *back on top of you?*" I asked before he could respond to my initial question.

"Yep."

I waited for him to say more, however his nonchalant nod was followed by nothing but silence. Gathering the sheet around my bare body to ensure I covered all the essential regions, I fully dismounted him ignoring the slight hesitation of my body to do so. While he sat up, leaning his back against the bed, I desperately searched my mind for any memory of last night.

I recalled working my shift at Alfonzo's Jazz Lounge & Bar and the run-in with my ex. I also recalled my girl-friends showing up and feeding me way too many shots to help *improve* my night, as they put it. But now for the life of me, I couldn't recall anything past that. And all attempts at regaining my memory immediately ceased when my eyes met Peyton's once more.

"Seriously, what are you doing here?" I questioned breaking the silence.

"Clearly visiting my brother," he stated.

"Pierre never mentioned anything to me about you coming."

He raised an eyebrow, the hint of a smile on his lips once again as he remained quiet, not rewarding me with a response. I guess in all honesty my surprise sounded some-what ridiculous since Pierre was his brother and by now, I should have been used to the newer version of Peyton doing whatever he wanted, whenever he wanted. Still, I had to ask, "What happened last night?"

"You don't remember?" he smirked.

"No, I do… I'm just asking again for shits and giggles?" The irritation seeping through my voice was irrefutable. I had a hammering headache. Gaps in my memory. A naked ass body. And he thought it was a good time to act cute.

"I'm not sure I've ever heard you say shit before," he snickered. "But then again, you've never been as sweet and innocent as everyone believed. Even if few people know that."

My eyes narrowed at his comment, I couldn't deny the twinge I felt at his words – *sweet* and *innocent*. They were titles I'd grown up being haunted by. Sugary, naive Hasani who always strived for perfection and never made any ripples for anyone. The type of woman who was everyone's friend, no one's enemy, and an occasional stranger's verbal punching bag. Going into a career as a concierge and bartender, only further emphasized my people pleasing reputation.

Peyton was right. Only a few of my closest friends ever truly knew me and he was on that list. Every other boss, friend – hell, even boyfriends – never saw past my good girl persona. Never saw the true me.

In my entire twenty-five years of being, I'd remained the perfect well-mannered daughter of divorced parents and loyal friend you could always count on to help you move. And if you needed an available shoulder to cry on, then you were in luck because I was your girl and I had two. I had amazing friends but staring across the room at Peyton made me realize that best friends were a rare commodity. And for a long time in my life, he was just that.

"Maybe we should get out there," he said breaking the standoff. There was shuffling coming from the hallway outside and we both knew who it had to be.

I nodded as he headed for the door revealing the t-shirt and light-weight jogging pants he'd been sleeping in. My eyes squinted at his attire wondering why I was the only one not wearing anything. Clearly reading my mind he added, "I couldn't get you back in your clothes."

"Okay, but how did they get off?" I inquired. "Did we have sex last night?"

The sexy smirk that slid across his face was as devilish as it was infuriating. He opened the door with my question lingering in the air, whispering, *"you were amazing"*, just before it shut.

CHAPTER TWO

Hasani

I found my clothes and purse neatly tucked away in the corner of the bedroom beside what I assumed was Peyton's open suitcase. Opening the drawers, I found half of his clothes inside, implying he'd be staying with Pierre for more than a night. And considering I was here a couple days ago and Pierre hadn't even mentioned Peyton's visit, then I wondered once again why he was here and why they hadn't told me.

After I took the wipes and Listerine strips from my purse, I gave my face and teeth a good once over. Although a bathroom would have been preferred, knowing both men were on the other side of the door meant I needed to look at least semi-decent before I left out. Grabbing my spare t-shirt and leggings from the drawer Pierre had given me, I glanced around the room hoping to spark my memory once more. But even through the blistering sunlight, nothing grew clearer.

"Hi, Sani Sunshine!" Pierre said the second I emerged from the bedroom.

Peyton was sitting on the bar stool with his back to me, while Pierre stood on the other side of the kitchen island holding a cup of water and two aspirin.

"Oh, my goodness, I've never loved you more," I moaned, taking the empty seat beside Peyton.

"Okay, Pie, maybe you can tell me what happened last night?" I probed after downing the pills and half of the cup of water. "Because Stone didn't say much."

Pierre smiled taking my phone out of his pocket. "Oh, honey, you left this little gem on the counter last night, and as you know, I have no boundaries. So, I watched all the videos you made." He let out a guilty sigh. "And can I just say, I am so proud of you."

My eyes grew bigger with each word he spoke, knowing that anything Pierre found gratifying and prideful, I would, in turn, find utterly shameful. And the fact that Peyton, who I hadn't seen in five years, also seemed to know everything about the past twelve hours that I was missing only further increased my anxiety.

"Okay, so I assume you remember your shift yesterday and calling me at around 7 P.M. to tell me that scum-of-the-earth—but still adequately hot—ex of yours showed up at Alfonzo's with his day of the week tramp, right?"

I nodded. "I didn't say any of it that way, but yes that's the gist."

"Sunshine, you're too nice. We already know this. You said Brandon showed up with a girl, other than the one he cheated on you with. Followed by him claiming that he had *mistakenly* shown up to the bar on your shift. Something we both know isn't true," he continued snapping his finger for added effect. My thoughts drifted as he spoke.

Last night…

"I'm sorry," Brandon exclaimed as soon as his date dipped off to the bathroom. "I didn't know you'd be here today."

"Right, because there's not a thousand other bars you could have gone to besides the one I work at." I adjusted the bottles of wine at the back of the bar, refusing to give him the satisfaction of my attention as he spoke.

"You know this became my favorite spot back when we were still together." He stretched out to touch my hand as I wiped down the bar. "Remember how many nights I'd sit in this very seat as you worked? And then we'd go back to your place or my place." I remained silent, pulling my arm away before he could reach me.

"Come on, Hasani, you know you miss me." The right corner of his mouth twisted up in a way I used to find attractive, but now saw it for the vindictive, cocky power trip it exposed. "We were together for over four years, making it through the college to real world shift and everything that came after. You don't just throw all that away because I made a mistake. It's been six months for goodness sake. Aren't you ready to forgive me yet?"

"Brandon, you cheated on me with my old college roommate. So please, spare me the sad eyes. Spare me the trips down memory lane. And just leave me alone. I should have ended things way before that and we both know it."

"You should have ended things? I treated you like a queen," he sneered. "You forgive everyone in your life for doing far worse, but you can't forgive me? Does that really seem fair?"

Slamming down the two drinks he'd ordered, I attempted to calm my nerves, hating the fact that I was still dealing with his shit. Not only was he one of the most manipulative people I'd ever met, but on top of that he lied far easier than telling the truth.

I'd known he and I weren't meant to be for months, but I'd still tried to make the situation work. Then one day, a little over six months ago, I found him cheating on me with my longstanding college roommate. He claimed it was only that one time, but she told me the truth about a month later; that it'd been going on for years.

Regardless of her confession, after I caught them in bed together the first time, I'd honestly been relieved. At last I had a strong reason to end it and assumed he'd finally just let me go. But now here he was trying to bait me. Only Brandon could show up at my job on a date, then try to still act like the good guy asking for me back the second she stepped away.

"I swear if you don't leave, I will have you thrown out," I threatened. "We're never getting back together, and I never need to see you again."

"You say that now Hasani, but we both know you'll forgive me. It's only a matter of time." Heeding my warning, he got up, meeting his date on her way back from the bathroom and headed for the exit.

After informing the team to never let him in again, I had called Pierre to recap the whole ordeal. He'd insisted on canceling his date to meet me, but I told him I had another hour on my shift and just wanted to go home and sleep it off.

Brandon wasn't dangerous but I hated him, and *hate* was a word I never used. Although Brandon had surely earned it, having taken advantage of my kindness more than anyone, in addition to showing up last night and proving even further what little respect he had for me. But that chapter in my life was done. I was over him and over our drama, remaining more upset at the fact that he refused to stay out of my life than by anything else he had done when he was still a part of it. A betrayal like his taught me important lessons, showed me I was stronger than people knew. And regardless of his continuous BS, I'd be just fine.

CHAPTER THREE

Hasani

"You remember all that, right?" Pierre asked, finishing his dictation of my encounter with my ex-boyfriend.

I sighed. "Yes, unfortunately."

Rehashing anything about Brandon was a waste of time, especially given that interaction was clearly one of the last parts I'd remembered. Turning to face Peyton, I stared at him for a few moments waiting for him to break the cool demeanor he'd sported since waking up. We hadn't seen each other in five years, but that couldn't discount our fifteen prior years of friendship. From middle school through high school, there was barely a moment I hadn't shared with either Pierre or Peyton. We were The Three Musketeers, bound early in life by our love for one another.

Peyton leaving after high school had marked the end of an era. He'd traveled to Spain, Italy, Africa, and a dozen other places chasing God knows what. He'd visited a couple times during our first two years of college and kept in touch when he could thereafter, but it wasn't quite the same as having him here and looking at him now.

As my gaze traveled the length of his body, I yearned to hear the untold stories resulting in every change that had occurred during our time apart. His hair was faded all the way around, except for short dreads coming from the top. The hairstyle surprisingly suited his naturally tamed eyebrows and strong jawline. However, instead of the clean-shaven look he once sported, he now rocked a short, nicely groomed beard that only further accentuated his features.

Rubbing his hands together was a tell of his, implying my staring was making him uncomfortable. A fact that only intensified as I admired the new tattoos streaming from his left hand, up his arm, and disappearing under the sleeve of his shirt. Peyton had always been attractive, but I wasn't entirely prepared for the allure of the sexy, rugged changes against his browned caramel complexion.

Turning my way, his gaze traced the length of me. Something I felt was unnecessary given our naked encounter earlier, but further made me question whether we'd slept together. My body ached, but not exactly in the pleasurable way I felt would come from a night with Peyton. A concept that intrigued me in ways that used to terrify me. Yet, my only hope now was that nothing had happened yesterday versus the possibility that I'd forgotten our time together entirely. And evidently there'd be no telling what really happened until my memory returned.

"You look good, Sani," Peyton said holding my gaze.

"You too, Stone."

Continuing our staring contest, I gently licked my lips,

drawing his eyes immediately downward. A reaction he recovered from as quickly as he'd faltered.

"Fuck-k," a voice quietly exhaled pulling our attention toward the direction of Pierre's bedroom. A spicy, shirtless man appeared, standing in the hallway.

Pierre rolled his eyes in the man's direction before glancing back at me and Stone. "Oh no, a bitch did not just open up his mouth and ruin a perfectly good eye fuck. I was getting wet just looking at the two of you."

And that's my gay best friend ladies and gentlemen. If all eyes hadn't been on me, I would have face palmed into my hand.

Peyton

As the guy walked over to Pierre, giving him a peck on the lips, it appeared Hasani wasn't the only one who'd missed something last night.

"Oh my damn, can we get them to do that again?" the man said. His voice was high and pitchy as he cheered us on, staring from Hasani to me like we were two actors on a television set awaiting our next cue. "And oh my damn, am I seeing double?"

The last question was directed solely at Pierre as he glanced from me to my brother.

"You are, but she's never looked at me that way," Pierre answered.

I laughed, shaking my head. Pierre and I were more than brothers, we were identical twins, who acted nothing alike. But that didn't stop us from being close our entire lives. He was the person I counted on more than anyone and I knew I was the same for him.

"Hi, I'm Hasani," she giggled extending a hand to the stranger standing beside Pierre.

"Hello, beautiful," he said accepting her hand. "I'm Elijah."

"Nice to meet you," Hasani smiled. "I guess your date went well?"

"Actually, I spilled a drink down Pierre's shirt during dinner," Elijah answered, his hands tracing down Pierre's fancy pajama top. "Luckily it turned out to be a blessing in disguise, because it finally got him to take me home and look at this gorge place!" Elijah twirled. "We may be gay, but I'm about to pull a full lesbian and move in tomorrow."

"Alright, slow your roll," Pierre interjected, gently grabbing Elijah's flailing arms.

While Elijah continued to stare at the three of us like his new best friends, I stole a glance back at Hasani. There was something different about her. Something I'd seen last night but dismissed as liquid courage. However, now in the sobering light of day, she was still sending me vibrations that dared me to push boundaries I had no right touching after all this time.

Forcing my attention back towards the group, I caught Pierre's eye. We weren't always the type of twins that read each other's minds, but the expression on his face was undeniable today. In addition to Elijah's flamboyant nature being a little too much for him this morning, there was a devious smirk plastered across Pierre's face. My brother could be *dramatic* himself at times, but he occasionally found it overwhelming in others. Though based on his current expression, he'd chosen to devote his attention elsewhere. As I silently urged him not to dive further into Hasani and me at the moment, he silently agreed to wait… for now.

"Alright, well now that everyone is acquainted it's time to jog more of Sani Sunshine's memory."

"Can't you just quickly tell me everything that happened last night?" she urged. "Rip off the Band-Aid?"

"Sorry honey, but no. This production is *wayyy* too good to waste," Pierre answered.

Trying to cover up my chuckle I was glad when Pierre continued.

"Being your bestie, I knew you weren't okay last night, so I sent the girls to meet you."

"I know. They took me to our spot in South Beach, nursing me with a drink and three shots… that I remember," Hasani replied, rubbing her forehead. "Then I've got nothing."

"Perfect." Placing the phone in her free hand, Pierre poured a round of mimosas before joining Elijah on the sofa beside us. "A shot with the girls and a couple rounds later is exactly where this starts. Press play!"

Last night…

I thought I was prepared to see Hasani again after all this time. But receiving a call from Pierre that he needed me to pick her up from some bar, when she didn't even know I was in town yet, was not a part of my plan. I had told Pierre not to tell her I was coming beforehand, since I wanted it to be a surprise. However, driving down the streets of Miami heading to see her had me wondering if I'd made the right choice.

It took over twenty minutes to find them in the crowded, triple level, tropical space that consisted of a restaurant on the bottom level and lounge on the top two. I only knew a couple of Hasani and Pierre's Miami friends, and being the social butterflies that they both were, there was no telling who she might be with. Therefore, spotting Krystal – one of their friends from back in college – was pure luck. As she led me to Hasani and the other girls, she warned me that the group was already pretty tipsy and two-shots-and-done Hasani was already six shots in.

I'd been laughing at Krystal's warning when the sight of Sani sucker punched me right in the gut and might have had me faltering my steps a bit if I hadn't have played it off. *There she is.* It was as though she was moving in slow motion as I watched her sway to the beat of the live band playing in the corner of the lounge. Most of her life, Hasani had kept her hair extremely straight and tamed, but the naturally curly afro with highlighted honey-blonde streaks barely touching her shoulders was nothing short of mesmerizing.

Laying eyes on Sani for the first time in five years hit me harder than I'd expected. I was taking in every view of her against the sultry, reggaeton setting, admiring the care-free way she was vibing with the music. Seconds later, Sani's dark-brown, doe-eyed gaze met mine and the room and people around me grew blurry, leaving only her in focus. The see-through, black, button-down top and distressed jeans she was wearing seemed to fall on every curve she possessed perfectly, further heightening her tawny skin tone and rosy lips. I knew she'd be happy to see me, especially in her tipsy state. But the way she was looking at me was unexpected, her lips piercing open into a soft smile, like she knew I was coming and had just taken awhile to get there.

Whether she was playing with my senses, or my own thoughts craved too loudly, for the first time I saw the woman she'd become instead of the girl I grew up with.

She was gorgeous. Uninhibited. Yet, as quickly as the excitement of her appearing happy to see me grew, it disappeared just as fast when I realized she might be mistaking me for my brother.

Pierre's hair was different than mine and he was cleanly shaven like I used to be. But she was under the influence of more alcohol than usual, so with he and I being twins she could easily overlook the differences. Once I grew closer, she opened her mouth to speak, watching me as I approached.

"Hi, Stone." Her voice sounded clear, like there was no mistaking me for my brother. I couldn't help the smirk that filled my face. And just like that, I felt sucker punched again.

CHAPTER FOUR

Peyton

"Seriously Pie! I took five shots in the first three videos alone. I danced on the bar like I was back in college and I sang karaoke in front of a crowd full of people at a non-karaoke bar." Hasani slammed the phone facedown. "I clearly blocked it out for my own good and watching these is making it so much worse."

"Maybe you just need a new perspective," Pierre responded. "Because it looks to me like my beautiful bestie finally let down her curls and had a much needed night on the town, making me incredibly proud."

"It wasn't that bad," I added, gently rubbing her arm after her head dropped to the countertop.

"How do you know that?"

Her head flew back up so abruptly, it startled me and knocked me off balance, causing my stool to shake beneath me.

"You watched these, too?"

"Not exactly." I hesitated, realizing she still didn't remember seeing me last night and hadn't reached those parts of the videos yet.

Letting out a sigh, she picked her phone back up. "I'm never drinking again."

"Oh, I second that," Krystal said, emerging from the bathroom.

"Kris, what the heck are you doing here?" Hasani yelled.

"I slept here," Krystal replied bashfully.

"Okay, but how'd you physically get here?"

"Um... I came with you two." Krystal pointed between me and Hasani. "Which clearly you don't remember."

I could see the frustration and embarrassment seeping through Sani's demeanor, her features growing even cuter under the scrutiny.

"Maybe you should keep watching," I said before their back and forth continued. "Then we can answer all your questions."

Last night...

"Ladies," I greeted.

Their booth was tucked into a section of the lounge with half a dozen plants surrounding it. Based on the empty bottle and lopsided smiles coming from the two women I hadn't met, it was clear Hasani wasn't the only tipsy one of the group.

"Hello sexy," one responded, earning her a light pat from Krystal. "What was that for?"

"Keep it in your pants," Krystal snapped.

"I'm wearing a dress K-r-y-s-t-a-l," the woman replied with an exaggerated head roll. "Besides I checked for a ring first unlike last time. See? Improvement!"

I'd heard her words but was still distracted by Hasani, who kept her eyes fixated on me. I opened my mouth to speak but was silenced when her friend grabbed my left hand, shaking it in front of the group ending her outburst by asking me whether or not I was single.

"Yes, I am," I smiled awkwardly. Women didn't usually make me nervous. But having Hasani's gaze hooked on me in a way I'd never seen before, was throwing me off my game.

"Told you," she stuck out her tongue. "I'm Chantall."

"So, what are you doing here?" Hasani asked cutting off Chantall's introduction to me.

"I'm here to get you."

"Okay, but what are you doing in Miami as a whole?"

"I have an art job in Wynwood, so I'll be staying through the rest of the month," I replied.

"Why didn't Pierre tell me?" she probed.

Her questions were sharp, although the direct, curious look on her face was something new I hadn't expected, but intriguingly liked.

"Aha! That's who he looks like," Chantall slurred as if she'd been questioning who I reminded her of since I'd arrived. "A more masculine, sexy, straight Pierre."

"That's because he's his identical twin brother, fool," Krystal interrupted, taking a seat on the opposite side of the booth.

Chantall frowned. "Okay, you're really snappy all of a sudden."

Krystal had always had an edge from what I could recall, similar to that of my brother. But she did seem even more short tempered, implying perhaps her drunkenness came out in different ways compared to that of her friends. Ignoring Chantall's comment, Krystal introduced me to the other woman in the booth and insisted on a final round before I took Hasani home.

"I don't believe it," Hasani whispered grabbing one of the strawberry daiquiris the waiter placed on the table.

"Is that Brandon? Your ex really can't take a hint," Chantall stated ironically. She'd been attempting to rub my leg for the past ten minutes, despite my constant removal of her hand. I was trying to be a gentleman, given that I didn't know her and she was obviously one of Hasani's friends. But I had zero interest in this woman and seriously wondered if the alcohol was the only thing to blame in her poor choice making.

"I'll handle it," I responded, instinctively rising from the booth.

I didn't hear Hasani get up behind me but was halted as she grabbed my arm. Turning me to face her, she gently placed her hand on my chest.

"Thank you, but he's my problem," she replied. "I'll be fine, Stone."

Even knowing the slight smile she shot me was forced, it set me at ease as I brushed a fallen curl out of her face. "I know you do," I whispered, silently hushing my savior complex. To be honest, I'd always felt that way about Hasani. Protective no matter the situation and ready to do whatever I had to do to keep her safe even if she could handle the situation on her own.

Returning to the table, all conversation ceased as we watched the interaction between Hasani and her ex. Krystal was recording them as we sat in silence, the girls cheering after Sani poured her daiquiri down the dude's lap. I'd heard stories about her ex, but never met him in person. And from the looks of it, that wouldn't be a factor in the future. However, if he made it a factor by coming around again, I would put him in his place myself.

He forcefully grabbed her wrist when she turned to walk away. I was halfway to them when she yanked free, followed by a swift punch to his nose. The hit didn't appear to be incredibly hard, but still sent him tumbling to the ground—proof that Hasani still had a mean right hook. Seeing her ex grab his nose brought a smile to my face as I reminisced about those self-defense lessons I used to give her in high school.

"Okay now I'm ready to go," Hasani huffed once I'd reached her. The view as she stood over him was a sight I wanted to capture and frame. As an artist, I'd always seen the parts of Sani that some didn't notice right away. Hasani was beautiful, strong *and* dominating.

"I got him good," she slurred, her eyes glazing over slightly as the altercation took the last of her sobriety.

"I've got you," I said, grabbing her waist to keep her steady. "Come on, ladies." I waved to them. "I'll take you all home."

Her ex had enough time to get up before the ladies reached us. But like the coward I already knew he was, he took one look at me and scurried away without a sound as soon as he found his legs.

CHAPTER FIVE

Hasani

The last of the videos ended with the girls and I all getting into Peyton's car, while Krystal and Chantall chanted, "*Rocky Rocky Rocky...*" over and over again. Slight memories returned as I watched the videos, but not all of them. There were still a lot of holes in the night that I wanted filled.

"Wasn't it amazing?" Elijah questioned eagerly the instant I closed the phone. "Felt like I was there, gurl! So, can I say that I don't even know your ex, but I got the cliff notes version and when your fist hit his face, I cringed and cheered all at once!"

Krystal and Peyton had been there last night and clearly Pierre and Elijah had already watched all the videos together. That left only me in the dark, shrinking as I swore I wouldn't do under their gaze, while everyone anticipated my response.

"I'm proud of you, sis," Pierre said squeezing my hand.

I forced a smiled as my mind began racing a mile a minute. "Thanks, but I think I need some air." People were popping out of rooms like Pierre's condo was a clown car headed to a fair. So, it was necessary that I left before even more people joined this *disclosure* party.

I'd walked four blocks before Peyton caught up with me.

"You okay?" he asked through the open window of his car.

"Yes, I'm fine," I huffed. "Except that I feel like all my friends know some secret I don't, including you who I haven't even seen in five years and just showed up out the blue the same night as my ex. Oh and to make matters worse, you somehow saw me naked and I can't remember what we did or if we did anything at all, causing me to completely spiral."

I hadn't intended on saying any of that out loud. Though I had to admit the word vomit I'd just spewed felt *so* good getting out. Not to mention I was proud of myself for speaking my mind, yet still having the forethought to hold back the part about me being attracted to him. A statement that would surely just make things further awkward at this given moment.

Peyton parked his car and joined me on the sidewalk, pulling me in for a hug I didn't know I needed.

"The evening got a little crazy for y'all, but nothing happened between us last night," he admitted.

"Then how come I was naked this morning? And why was I at Pierre's place instead of my home."

"We couldn't get Krystal to wake up after dropping off the other two women. So you suggested I take y'all to Pierre's place instead since your apartment is much smaller and you felt she'd be more comfortable on his couch."

I could feel my heartbeat grow calmer as he stroked my arms while he spoke.

"You stripped on your way to the guest bedroom. I didn't see anything...until this morning," he laughed. "Nothing bad happened to you at all. I wouldn't let it."

His words rang through my head like the sweetest melody, relieving my tense muscles. *Nothing happened. I guess the videos did tell me most of the story after all.*

"Do you want me to take you home?" he asked.

I lifted my eyes to meet his. "Yes." I had fully intended on immediately retreating to the car so he could indeed take me home. But as if on cue, his wrists slowed their up and down motion, a wave of heat rushing between us. Within seconds, the staring contest was back on, but it was one I could feel myself losing as I fought the urge to touch his lushly full lips.

He opened his mouth to speak twice, but nothing came out. On his third attempt his mouth barely inched open before my own cascaded towards him, not stopping until my lips encountered his. He tasted savory, like a hint of pineapple mixed with a peppery spice I couldn't quite place. I didn't need to know the flavor though to realize that one taste was enough to get me hooked.

When one of his hands wrapped around my waist before the other slid behind the nape of my neck, I slowly rolled my tongue into his. Taking in Every. Single. Bit. I recalled girls over the years talking about how good of a kisser Peyton Stone was, but I'd never experienced kissing him firsthand. And now that I had, I couldn't agree with them more.

Pulling away wasn't something I liked doing. Yet, his kiss had released something inside of me, bringing my memories flooding out like a freshly de-corked champagne bottle, ready to explode.

"I remember," I whispered.

Last night…

"She is out for the count," I giggled, laying a blanket over Krystal after Peyton placed her on the couch.

"Yeah, you ladies went hard tonight. I'm surprised you're still awake," Peyton replied.

"I'm sure once the adrenaline wears off, I'll pass out just like Kris."

"Looks like Pierre still isn't back from his date," he said, closing Pierre's bedroom door before returning to the front room. "I still can't believe he has so many plants around this place. He used to hate when you'd make him be outside gardening all day."

I smiled. "Yeah I remember, but I take care of most of these beauties myself. It's good for Pie to have the plants around him, even if he disdains taking care of them himself."

Grabbing a water from the fridge, I joined Peyton on the floor in front of the fireplace. "I started an urban gardening group down here after we graduated. It's only been a couple years but it's really growing."

"I'm not surprised. You've always had a green thumb." He tossed me a pillow. "I thought you'd make a business out of plants someday. Become a landscape architect or something."

"I do like the sound of that," I replied glaring up at the coved ceiling. Peyton and I were falling right back into our routine with conversation flowing as easily as water down a clear stream.

"Do you remember back in high school when you got

the entire cheerleading squad and basketball team to volunteer four weekends straight to rebuild the town's square after that bad storm destroyed it?" he asked. "It was clear then that you loved it."

"As I recall, you had a lot to do with them helping out. Since you were the captain of the basketball team, all I had to do was convince you and everyone else fell in line."

"I'm sure that wasn't too hard for you. I would always do anything you asked," he smirked. "Besides you were dating the other co-captain, so the rest of the team really didn't stand a chance."

Laying on the rug beside Peyton listening to him talk about our past, I had three revelations. The first of which being that I had really missed his voice. You'd think he and Pierre would sound the same being identical twins and all, but they didn't. His voice was deep and heavy, reflecting everything the world had put him through. Both he and Pierre had endured a lot, but Peyton always bore the brunt of it for the both of them.

"Did that bother you?" I asked. "Me dating him?" I almost shook my head at my own blunt question. *Why in the world did I ask him that?*

He shrugged, running a hand through his hair. "It's not right for me to say *yes*. We were all friends."

Humph. Not the answer I'd expected but observing him brought me to the second discernment. He'd changed quite a bit over the years. His style now was that of a rugged, yet vogueish artist versus a basketball player. Everything from his hair to his tattoos, and even the chosen layering of his clothes was a flair all his own.

"Yeah, but you, me and Pierre were always more than just friends," I reflected. "With your parents all but disowning him for being who he is, you never wavered in your decision to choose him over the rest of your family."

He clenched his jaw. "It shouldn't have been a choice that had to be made."

I could hear the anger seep through his voice, although I knew it wasn't directed at me. "No, it shouldn't have. But regardless of that, you really stepped up and became more like an older brother to him than his twin."

"So, did you. Stepping up that is," he countered. "Without your mom being so great and having us over for dinner almost every night, I'm not sure how things would have turned out for us. Pierre and I had each other, but you were our other rock. How else would we have become *The Three Musketeers*, as Pierre used to call us?"

I smirked, hoping that Peyton couldn't see the third insight I'd had in seeing him tonight. *Lust*. It wasn't just about how handsome Peyton looked. It was also the way he carried himself and spoke to me tonight. He'd always been confident—occasionally cocky. But the assuredness in his words was the most alluring new quality that I hadn't known he possessed. Either that or I'd never allowed myself to fully focus on it before.

"Sani, you always had your friends, the cheerleading squad and your parents, even after the divorce. And I always had my boys, basketball, and art. But Pierre… Pierre only had the two of us. I could never risk him losing that."

"Neither could I," I agreed. "But Stone, we're not kids anymore and Pierre is more than okay now. So I have to ask, where does that leave your feelings for just me?"

He swallowed hard at yet another one of my blunt questions but remained silent, undoubtedly pondering what I'd asked. It may have seemed candid to him, but my own thoughts had been urging me to ask from the moment I saw him in the bar. Despite my lousy ex showing back up and Chantall throwing herself at Peyton, there'd been something thick in the air between the two of us. And I wanted to know what it meant to him.

"I asked myself that same question six months ago when I heard about your breakup."

I longed for him to keep speaking, but instead he paused. I was afraid he would just stop there, before he finally began talking again.

"When you and Pierre left for school, it gave me the breather I needed to see who I was outside of being his protector and twin. And as it turned out, the art hobby I'd picked up to cope with everything that went on with our parents was more of a passion than I originally thought."

"Taking you to Europe and all the other places in the world you've seen," I added with a half-smile.

He beamed. "Exactly. I worked with other street artists in London and Prague. I saw the pyramids, Victoria Falls, and discovered a dozen other places I'd love to show you one day. But most importantly, I found myself, as cheesy as it sounds."

"I never had any doubts," I replied once I was sure he'd finished. I'd kept up with his work over the years and was proud at what he'd accomplished. Turning street art into a profession. "You know the mural you did back home is still up to be admired by everyone."

"Yeah, your mom told me you petitioned the town to have it declared a historical wall." He laughed.

"Of course, she did." I shook my head in slight embarrassment. I didn't intend on telling him I'd had any part in turning the wall into a landmark since we hadn't seen each other in years, and it might've seemed strange that I cared so much about it. But I should have known my mother would give me up anyways. "Well, I was just looking out for my own time investment since I did spend *days* there as you perfected every little detail."

"Well since my best friend was the one who gave me my first art set, and then kept me company for *days* while I painted, then it needed to be good." He stood up rather abruptly, returning with a sketchbook. "Remember how I said I was in town to do a mural in Wynwood?" He handed me the open book. "Here's my idea."

My eyes lit up immediately. "This is *amazing*." I ran my fingers down the drawing taking in every minute detail. "I can't wait to see it in its full view."

His mouth churned up into a grin before falling into a soft smile. "I can't wait for you to see it, either."

"You know in all my travels, you're still the most caring, thoughtful person I've met," he continued, pushing that same unruly curl from earlier out of my face. "But you're also stubborn and strong-willed, even though society and those closest to you can overlook it. You see people in ways they don't always see themselves. Growing up, I know you always saw Pierre and I for the individuals we were, without comparing us like so many people tended to do."

Playing with the sleeve of his shirt I took in his words. "I loved you both for your differences."

I was sure he understood the way I meant it, but when the look in his eyes flickered from caring to seductive, my breath caught in my throat silencing any further words. We could have been there for days. Hours. Minutes. Each second growing longer than the last. Until I felt his lips on mine in one needy swoop.

He commanded my mouth before I could even comprehend what was happening. It was our *first* kiss. A kiss that had been years in the making. A kiss covered in the passion and familiarity of knowing each other the way that we did.

As our lips grew more daring, it felt as if each nibble held every missed prom invite and lost date. Every wrong first kiss and wasted relationship. Every experience we could have shared together, but instead spent with someone else. It was all here in this kiss. Heavily tantalizing my weary mind.

I didn't want it to end, but he placed one final kiss on my lips before pulling away.

"I think we should stop and talk about this again when you're completely sober."

I blinked a few times, trying to shake myself from his lust-filled fog. "Whatever you say, Stone," I finally replied getting up from the rug. I stripped on my way to the guest bedroom, leaving pieces of my clothes like breadcrumbs leading to the bed. I wanted him to follow. I wanted more. But he was right.

When he finally did emerge in the room, covering his eyes until I told him I was securely under the sheets, I felt safe. Safer than I'd felt in a long time. Safe enough to close my eyes and drift off to sleep.

CHAPTER SIX

Peyton

We drove in silence, our thoughts consuming the moment as both kisses we'd shared hung in the air on invisible strings ready to be pulled. Strings that appeared to be just outside our reach, taunting us with yearning.

When we arrived at her apartment, she quickly entered, leaving me standing in the open doorway with nothing but the stillness to direct me. I wasn't sure how she was feeling, but I hoped I'd read the sentiment correctly in staying.

I grabbed a Vitamin Water from the fridge while she disappeared into what I assumed was her bathroom. Her place was cozy and colorful. Exactly what I'd expected. She had art in every corner, including a couple pieces I'd made back in high school.

I can't believe she kept these, I thought, flowing from the sculptures to the photographs outlining her walls. She had a photo of the three of us with her mom, along with one of her dad and half-siblings. But as the pictures traveled from childhood to adulthood, I ceased to be in them.

I knew why. It'd been my choice after all, not to go to university with her and Pierre, and in turn, lose out on everything that followed. Yet the pining feeling that was starting to develop, seeing my decision displayed in front of me as happy memories I'd wasted, didn't sit entirely easy.

When the bathroom door creaked open, I remained fixated on the wall of photographs.

"Like what you see?" she asked.

"Your pictures are beautiful," I answered. "I'm happy I made the board at all given how long it's been."

"Thanks, but that's not what I meant."

Turning to face her, I nearly dropped the water bottle as she approached wearing nothing but a towel. Her hair was pulled up into a curly pouf, while her skin glistened from the areas that were still damp.

"I'd already started taking a shower before realizing how lonely it was being alone under the steamy water," she said.

"Is that right?" I retorted, barely able to formulate words as she stopped less than an inch out of reach. I could hardly swallow as I stared at her, this territory between us new and unexplored before last night.

"Yes." The sexy grin on her mouth begged to be kissed away. But as she took control of the moment, I leaned back awaiting her next move.

"If you come any closer, there'll be no turning back," I warned, feeling my urges taking hold. "I've denied myself of your taste for so long, it won't be a one and done. I'll want more."

Closing the gap between us, she brought her lips to my ear and whispered, "Then take me."

She'd never have to tell me twice. Holding back last night had been near impossible, and now that I had a second chance, there was no way in hell I was going to waste it. Pulling her sexy mouth to mine, I devoured her sweet taste. Starting with her lips, then moving to her tongue, challenging it to tussle against my own. And battle she did, each movement having a satisfying reaction more potent than the last.

Our kiss last night had been filled with certain admissions, causing me to wonder what might have been had we crossed that line sooner. But we made the choice not to for Pierre's sake, and no choice made out of love should be regretted. Therefore, from this moment forward I silently vowed to focus on our future and not our past. Every kiss and every first with Hasani would become a part of our new story. All beginning today.

"Don't stop," she whispered breathlessly, when I pulled away gently, her breath playing with my senses.

Gripping both thighs, I lifted her in the air, leaving her towel in place. "This is only the start," I said in between kisses as I carried her to the couch, placing her on my lap as I sat down.

I craved tasting her other lips, but she was already making quick work of freeing my dick from my pants, causing him to jump at the thought of being inside her. I dipped one finger into her center, breaking off our kiss just long enough to pull my shirt over my head. She was already so wet, causing me to grow harder until her fingertips abruptly slowed to trace the tattoos on my arms and chest.

"They're like a roadmap of your life," she sighed. "So many I've never seen, each with their own story."

"I'll tell you about them later," I replied. "And I've got plenty of room for new ones."

Slowing my lust long enough to take in her vulnerable gaze, I observed the way her eyes lingered on my numerous tatts. They were art I'd chosen carefully to mark different parts of my life. From my broken family, to the experiences that had helped me heal, they indeed told my story. However, there was one part of my puzzle missing. A part I'd come to Miami hoping Hasani might fit. "I've got plenty of room to fill with our important experiences," I explained, "Because I didn't come back to Miami just for my art, I came back for you. To finally give us a chance."

It was one of the most honest statements I'd made in a very long time, leaving me defenseless against her. I patiently waited for her response, gently massaging her neck as her eyes peered up revealing her tearful gaze.

"Do you promise?" Her voice quivered with hope as she leaned her forehead against mine.

"I promise," I answered, relief easing my tension as I guided her delicate lips toward mine.

I wanted to comfort her and give her what she needed even if that meant ignoring my own desires for the time being. But Hasani once again proved she was my perfect woman, when she intensified our kiss, removing her towel in the process.

Admiring her beautifully naked curves, I cupped her right breast in my hand before popping her nipple into my mouth. I'd never had a moment turn from sweet to sinful in such a short span of time. But I was coming to realize that with Sani, nothing would be as I'd experienced with past women.

She let out an intense moan that didn't subside even after I gave her other breast equal attention. I wanted to savor her, but I knew deep down that we'd have time for that. I wasn't lying earlier when I told her there'd be no turning back and I'd want more. But for now, I needed to be *inside* her, and hearing her ask for the same left nothing further to consider.

Lifting her up, I fully released my dick, allowing me to slide into her sweet center as I slowly placed her back down.

"Stone," she whimpered. Her groan becoming high pitched as it mixed with my own animalistic grunt. Each thrust bringing me deeper and deeper inside of her.

As she took over the motion, riding me until she'd taken in every inch, I could feel her wetness increase as she approached a climax years in the making. We had not spent all this time just pining for one another. We'd grown into individuals we could both be proud of and we were at peace with that.

But now, this was finally our time together. Two people ready to walk the same path and finally see where it led. Discover what more we could mean to one another, while helping fulfill each other's desires in more ways than one. Plus, with a history like ours, and a passion unfaded, there was no telling what we could become.

EPILOGUE

Hasani

Six months later…

"This place is beautiful," my mom said, giving both Peyton and me a tight squeeze.

"Thank you, Mom, we couldn't be happier with the outcome," I replied. "I'm so proud of him."

"Says the woman who made all this happen," Peyton interjected before my mom got pulled away by another friend of the family.

"Running this outdoor art gallery, focused on street art with you is exactly what I wanted. The way you designed the landscape to flow with the pieces is just perfect," he continued, "and there's no one I'd rather do this with than you."

Placing a quick peck on my lips, Peyton got called away

by a couple of other street artists hoping to display their work in our gallery.

"Girl, can you please tell me he's actually a triplet and not just a twin?" Chantall blurted the second he was out of earshot as she and Krystal approached. Not that it would have mattered to her if Peyton had overheard. Chantall was certainly not the shy type and she rarely got embarrassed.

"Sorry Cha Cha, but it's only the two of them," I answered.

Krystal rolled her eyes in dismissal and prompted me to drop some much-needed tea for Cha Cha. "You know, Kris actually asked him on a date back when we were in university together."

"*What*?" Pierre yelped, stealing Chantall's thunder. I hadn't even seen him sneak up. "You asked out my brother?" He lightly slapped her on the arm. "Why didn't I know about this?"

"Probably because he said he *couldn't* go and unlike some people in this group, I can keep a secret." Krystal scowled, glancing at Chantall. "Besides, I asked him out after meeting him with Pierre and wayyy before I saw the way he and Hasani stared at each other like they could remove the other's clothes just with their eyes. He was sexy and all, but alas, we were not meant to be, as he was destined for a life of dreamy-eyed, nauseating stares."

"But you still find it necessary to give me shit for admiring his attributes, when clearly you already did, too," Chantall said, unaffected by Krystal's sarcastic humor.

Krystal gave her a sassy smirk. "Yeah, but I did it with class."

"Ladies, ladies! Please don't fight over Peyton who is taken with Miss Sani Sunshine over here." Pierre shouted. "Instead fight over me. The cuter twin."

We all giggled, both Krystal and Chantall realizing how stupid the argument was. Neither of them truly wanted Peyton, nor would they ever cross that line because of me. They were my ride-or-die girls, but it seemed they often fought just to fight. They were complete opposites and despite me loving them for it, they often clashed because of it.

Waving down a server, I grabbed four champagnes from his tray of drinks and handed one to each of my three friends.

"So now that that's over, because y'all know I would cut a bitch for my man," I said jokingly, "I'd like to give a toast for each of you.

"Thank y'all for always being there for me and seeing me through this grand opening for *The Art of Love Gallery*. We plan on being a staple here in Wynwood for many years to come and I truly couldn't have done it without my three closest friends. I love you bitches."

Pierre grinned and Krystal and Chantall both pretended to dab their eyes.

"See, and here I thought I was your closest friend," Peyton teased, joining us.

"Well yet another thing you're wrong about," Pierre jabbed, slapping him on the back.

"You are responsible for this potty mouth of Sani's though," Krystal added, wrapping her free hand around Pierre's waist as a sign of solidarity.

"Nope, that's all her," Peyton countered. "I keep telling her that dirty mouth will get her in trouble one of these days."

"Is that right, Stone?" I teased. Leaning closer to him to ensure no other gallery attendees could overhear, I whispered, "And here I thought you liked it dirty."

Instead of responding, he kissed me so quickly I barely

had time to react. And just like a bestie, Pierre grabbed my champagne glass before I dropped it.

"That is way too much for my single ass," I heard one of them say, but I didn't care. Peyton Stone was my boyfriend, business partner, and future husband if I had anything to say about it. We just worked together and becoming a *we* had indeed been a long time coming.

THE END

ABOUT KELSEY GREEN

I'm a travel and video enthusiast with a BS in Civil Engineering. However, when I'm not wearing my engineering hat, I can be found expressing myself through visual artistry.

Whether videos, novels or poetry are your jam, I enjoy diving into the world around me to see beneath the surface and capture the raw beauty furthermore translating my vision through words and filmic innovation.

I've been journaling since I was a young girl, so I only found it natural to begin penning stories that reflect the emotion only previously portrayed in my videos. I'm a published author and poet, who enjoys depicting life's adventure's through suspenseful plots and romantic storylines. So I hope you'll join me on this therapeutic adventure of expression and imagination by diving into my work.

For more information, visit her website at www.barewithkels.com

facebook.com/authorkelseygreen

twitter.com/nicoledolls67

instagram.com/nicoledolls67

ALSO BY KELSEY GREEN

Contemporary Romance

The Renegade Bid

Mutually Exclusive

Mystery

The Desert Never Tells

Horror Romance

The Undead

Poetry

I Am King

STUCK WITH YOU

KIMMIE FERRELL

Landon only has ten days to show Gianna he's not the man she thinks he is. But the uphill battle to win her heart is not easy. As the two rival event planners work to pull off the wedding of the century, they realize sometimes the best kind of love is unplanned.

Dedicated in loving memory of Kimberly Ferrell. Ma, I know you're smiling down at me, glad I FINALLY finished something. Thanks for your unwavering support. We love & miss you.

CHAPTER ONE

Gianna

"I hope he trips and falls, hits his head against the concrete, and forgets that he's such an arrogant asshole. Ol' entitled ass jerk."

I ignored the wide-eyed stares as I made my way through the lobby of the Wolf Creek Inn at Brewer Creek Lake, successfully dodging the hordes of guests milling around. Unlike them, I had places to be and things to do. I shifted the heavy binder tucked under my arm, then pressed a finger to the earpiece to better hear over the symphony of conversations floating around me.

"Or better yet, since his head and ego are so big, I hope he flies far, far away straight into some power lines, a plane, or even the side of a building."

"You're sick and twisted," my best friend and business partner Delaney said. I could hear the hint of disapproval in her tone, though it didn't faze me one bit.

"At least I didn't get suckered into the family's business after being threatened with being cut off by mommy dearest."

Delaney gasped. "Gi, you don't know that for sure."

And the truth was? I didn't. I had no logical reason to know why a man like Landon Wilson, an entitled playboy with a revolving door of women and more money than his Ivy League education could teach him how to count, would be interested in his family's event planning business but I strongly believed he hadn't done so on his own accord.

"You're right, I don't," I agreed. "I'm surprised Josephine Wilson allowed someone like Landon to run a branch of A Wilson Affair. Chances are he'll run it straight into the ground, which would be a great thing for us."

Delaney and I were the owners of Splendid Soirees, an event-planning company out of Ellington, Maryland. As far as businesses went, we did all right, amazing even. Until the Wilsons brought their nationally recognized company, A Wilson Affair, to Dixon, Maryland, seven miles from the Splendid Soirees' offices. Hence the reason why I cursed Landon every chance I got.

But things hadn't always been like this between us.

Landon and I'd met ten months ago at an anniversary party I'd planned for his godparents—a fun fact I hadn't known until after his mother disrespected me by calling me the help. From the moment I'd laid eyes on him, I'd wanted him. Point blank period. No sugarcoating it or beating around the bush. Smooth toffee-colored skin free of blemishes, dark brown eyes, thick curly hair faded on the sides that gave him a rugged yet professional look, full lips, eyelashes women like me would kill for, and a sculpted body chiseled to perfection. Landon Wilson was a wet dream brought to life. And for a few brief minutes, after he

walked over to me and introduced himself, I'd contem-
plated leaving the event early with him.

We'd spent some of the evening talking when I wasn't
putting out fires. I'd learned we had quite a bit in common,
but before Landon and I could exchange numbers and set
a date and time for the dinner date he'd asked me on, we
were approached by his mother. By most standards,
Josephine Wilson was stunning, with old classic Hollywood
beauty, full of grace and poise. Still, she lacked manners.
And seeing her youngest son fraternizing with me easily
brought out the ugly side no amount of makeup applied
could hide.

Delaney groaned, forcing my attention to the phone
call. "Seriously, stop. You shouldn't say things you don't
know are true. You never know who's listening. Aren't you
on a date, anyway?"

"Yep," I lied, hoping Delaney didn't pick up on my
nervousness. Tonight, I had a meeting with Splendid
Soirees' newest client, but because of the confidentiality
clause in our contract, Delaney was permitted from knowing. "But back to the topic at hand. Landon Wilson is a
jerk."

"You've mentioned that, but you haven't told me what
he did this time."

I scoffed. "Your sentence shouldn't even be ending in
'this time.' I'm tired of him." I had a long laundry list of
reasons why I despised Landon Wilson, including my
attraction to him, but I couldn't tell Delaney this info.
"What? Besides him ordering the last Danish Apple Puff
from Amber's Café this morning or calling the tow
company after I parked in front of his office while I ran
inside the store? Hang on, I'll show you what he did." I
swiped the screen of my phone, unlocking it, and
forwarded Delaney the message I'd received from Landon

moments ago. Less than a minute later, my phone vibrated in my hand. Confused, I glanced at the image of Delaney's face plastered on my screen. Swiping it, I connected the Duo video call.

"So, you're mad because he sent you a copy of his interview?"

"Yes, Laney! Landon's rubbing it in our faces. Look at who his mama is. Josephine Wilson is like the black, female version of David Tutera. Everyone knows about A Wilson Affair."

Delaney shook her head. "I get why you're mad, Gianna, but you have to let it go. A Wilson Affair is here to stay, and the best thing for us—no you—to do is continue to focus on building Splendid Soirees. We might not be a household name, but we've got a helluva clientele. Jonquis came to us when planning his proposal, not AWA."

"You're right. It's..." I snapped my mouth close, acutely aware of someone watching me. The fine hairs sprinkled on my arms and at the back of my neck stood on end. I scanned the room for the source of the dread coiling my stomach. Only one person could make me feel this way: the thorn in my side, the bane of my existence, also known as The World's Most Irritatingly Sexy Man—holding the title since his becoming of age—Landon Wilson. Chances were, Landon was probably as irritating now as he was in his mama's womb.

After a few seconds of searching, I found Landon standing near a water fountain. Our eyes connected, sending a tremor of awareness straight through me. The corners of his mouth curved into a smirk powerful enough to liquify panties. Landon nodded his head in a greeting and winked.

"Laney, I gotta go. I'll call you once I get home." After

exchanging goodbyes, I slipped my phone into my purse and glanced at Landon once more.

"I can't stand his ass," I mumbled, continuing to my destination, but the hardening of my nipples and the butterflies in my stomach suggested something different.

CHAPTER TWO

Landon

Most people would be offended if they had overheard someone calling them every name in the insult dictionary, but not me. Everything Gianna said was absolutely true. Well, most of it anyway. Arrogant? Check. Entitled? Check. Asshole? Check. Suckered into the family business after being threatened with being cut off by Mommy Dearest? I'd give her half a check for that one but she wasn't too far off. "Suckered" would insinuate I'd been duped. I hadn't. "Threatened", which was more of an ominous indication of intent, was more accurate as my trust fund had been frozen until I acquiesced.

See, Gianna wasn't so far off.

I didn't consider myself a soft ass dude who couldn't take being told about himself. I grew up with people who talked about you behind your back and smiled in your face, and you considered them friends. I'd grown accustomed to it. The smack talk coming from Gianna Johnson felt more like a compliment than an insult because I knew the truth behind her "hatred" for me.

She was attracted to me.

I'd known it from the moment I caught her staring at me almost eleven months ago. I'd read the desire and pure unadulterated lust in her big, expressive brown eyes. But she definitely wasn't alone in this thing. I wanted Ms. Gianna Johnson. What able-bodied man wouldn't be attracted to her? Five-seven, smooth milk chocolate skin, doe-shaped eyes, full lips, thick hips and thighs, hips for days, and an ass I would use as a pillow if she were in my bed. But Gianna had a lot more going for her other than her looks. Hard-working, caring, intelligent with a wicked sense of humor, and unique were all traits I associated with Gianna.

I pushed the thoughts of Gianna out of my head to get my mind right for my meeting with my newest clients to plan their million-dollar affair. I'd worked on several events since being forced to take over the Dixon office of A Wilson Affair, but nothing of this magnitude. A lot was riding on the success of this event. Yes, I wanted access to my trust fund, but I also had to prove I wasn't the screw up my parents labeled me since I'd quit my job as an accountant to follow my dreams to be a photographer. Even Gianna, who I'd only met briefly, believed I would run the Dixon office straight into the ground.

"Not if I can help it." I opened the door to Luigi's and stepped inside, immediately assaulted by the delicious aromas wafting through the air. My stomach growled, reminding me I hadn't had anything to eat since lunchtime and I was long overdue. At the host stand, I gave the young man my name.

"Good evening, Mr. Wilson. I've been expecting you.

Unfortunately, since all the members of your party have not checked in, I cannot see you to your table. However, you can visit the bar, and once your guest arrives, I can get you."

"Sounds good." As I headed over to the bar, my eyes widened at the sight of Gianna leaning against the bar top. Her black high-low dress clung to her body, outlining the mouth-watering curves of her hips and ass. A pair of black strappy high heels accented those incredibly long, toned legs of hers I'd envisioned one too many times wrapped around my waist or perched on my shoulders. As if sensing my perusal, Gianna turned around, groaned, then returned her attention to the bartender as he placed a drink in front of her.

"I would ask if you're following me, but it's pointless since a stalker would always say…"

Gianna threw a hand up to silence me. "I don't know what you want, but keep it to yourself. I'm not in the mood to deal with you and your inflated ass ego."

My eyes damn near popped out my head. "Damn, Gigi."

Gianna's gaze remained locked on the television screen in front of her, but her jaw clenched. The only indication I'd gotten to her. "And I asked you to stop calling me Gigi. This is why we have nothing to talk about." She finally turned to face me. "Besides, if memory serves me correctly, you said everything you needed to ten months ago."

"Look, Gianna—"

"Excuse me, Mr. Wilson. Ms. Johnson," a voice interrupted. "I'm Janet, I have a meeting with you both."

Hopping from the stool, Gianna greeted the woman with a hug. "Janet, it's so wonderful to see you again. How have you been?"

"Doing well, Gianna. How about you? Has Splendid

Soirees seen an influx of new clients since Jonquis tagged you on his IG?"

"We have, although I'm sure our competitors wish we didn't. Especially since they've been trying to steal them all." Gianna cut her eyes my way.

"Now, Gigi, you know I'm a lover, not a thief."

Ignoring my remark, Gianna stepped past me. "Janet, you're meeting us both?"

Janet nodded. "Yep. I can explain more once we take our seats."

We were escorted through the restaurant to a semi-private room in the back. After taking our seats and ordering drinks—I chose a whiskey neat—Janet smiled at us both. "I know you're both confused, so I'm going to jump right in and say it. I'm the personal assistant for R&B superstar, Jonquis Samson, who recently became engaged to rap star, Azura."

Everyone knew who Jonquis Samson and Azura were. They were the reigning queen and king of Hip-Hop and R&B. I'd had the pleasure of working with Azura several times before as her photographer.

"I'm sure I speak for Gi—Ms. Johnson—when I say it's unusual to schedule a meeting with two planners from different companies at the same time."

"It is, Mr. Wilson." Before she could continue, the waiter appeared with our drinks and disappeared. "However, they want both of you to plan their nuptials."

"What? You're kidding, right?" Gianna and I asked at the same time.

"No, I'm not." Janet removed two stacks of paper from her briefcase and pushed them in front of us. "While vacationing here, Jonquis proposed. And because they both loved the area, they decided that they want to get married here." Janet glanced between us. "You've both worked with

Jonquis and Azura and they trust you. Given the circumstances, it's needed."

"And those are?" From experience, I knew this was where the bomb got dropped, and judging from the silence coming from my right, Gianna had braced herself, too.

"The wedding will be held in two weeks."

"Two weeks," I yelled. Gianna gasped loudly.

"Actually, eleven days." Before either of us could comment, Janet rushed on. "Yes, there are time restraints and I guarantee you both will be compensated well. There are a few more stipulations in place. To prevent details from being leaked to the public, you'll be asked to sign another non-disclosure agreement. I know you've signed one before this meeting. However, this contract is required by the network."

"Network?"

"Yes, Mr. Wilson. The couple negotiated a deal to have their wedding televised in an eight-episode special leading up to it. I'm sure you both know there are already rumors concerning this event being published online. However, since you're both well-known planners in the area, having you both run around Brewer Creek Lake with a camera crew following you would look suspicious."

I agreed but still wondered how the footage of the planning process would be recorded. I didn't have to wait long for an answer.

Janet took a sip of her drink, her lips curved into a side smirk. "You'll both be required to stay at the cabin where the event will take place together, and it's been outfitted with cameras to record your every move."

CHAPTER THREE

Gianna

"Why did I even agree to do this shit?"

I glared at my reflection in the rearview mirror, as if waiting for an answer I already knew. It was the same response anyone gave when asked why they signed up to be on reality television shows? For the exposure. It had been the reason I'd snatched the contract Janet placed in front of me and signed my name on the highlighted lines on each of the fifteen pages. As a reality TV junkie, I knew the appeal of shows like Love & Hip-Hop and Real House-wives. I understood why people wanted to keep up with the Kardashians. Regular people enjoyed seeing our favorite celebrities doing everyday things like walking the dog while talking on the phone with a designer in Milan, wearing custom red bottoms.

Wedding specials were the same thing. Cameras catching the bride, bridesmaids, wedding planner, and sometimes the groom, ripping and running around town, sitting through meetings with the linen company debating which table runner was lilac, choosing slipcovers, chair styles, tablecloths, napkins, and silverware. It was pretty dull stuff. Hence the reason I couldn't understand the need to have a cameraman following me. This whole situation was starting to feel a lot less like me planning a wedding and a lot more like a season of The Real World.

This is a true story of two rival event planners, who'll live together in a log cabin. Hired to work on the social event of the year and have their lives taped. Find out what happens when they stop playing nice and get real. The Real World: Brewer Creek Lake.

I leaned my head back against the headrest of my midsize sedan and closed my eyes. "You can do this, Gi. Remove the keys from the ignition, undo your seatbelt, and open the door. Once you've done those three things, getting out of the car, unloading your bags, and going into the house will be a breeze."

If only I believed those words.

Nothing about the next ten days would be a breeze. Not planning a million dollar wedding from the confines of a cabin in the middle of the woods, while keeping this a secret from my business partner and best friend thanks to the confidentiality agreement, nor having to surrender all my personal electronics. And definitely not being forced to endure the man now standing on the front porch with his hands tucked into the pockets of his gray sweatpants.

Why does he have to look so damn sexy?

Since learning I would be required to live with Landon while planning Jonquis and Azura's wedding, I'd dreaded this moment where we'd have to be alone together. Each time I came into contact with him, I remembered every-thing his mother had said—and subsequently did. It was one thing to believe your son deserved a woman whose social status matched his own. But to disrespect, degrade, and denounce someone because of it was another.

I mean, being honest, I knew Landon played in a league of his own before he even introduced himself. He'd carried himself with an air of self-confidence I'd only seen in lawyers, doctors, and celebrities. He had a chip perched on his shoulder and an enormous ass ego, but for him, it worked. His arrogance made him even more appealing. Immaculately dressed, handsome, intelligent, with the kindest brown eyes I'd ever gazed into, he was a winning combination in anyone's book. In the time I'd spent talking to Landon, I'd learned enough about him to expect him to be the kind of man who stood up for himself and those around him.

But he didn't.

After his mother called me the help once again—and a couple other insults I tried hard to forget—Landon smooth walked away, leaving me to take the vile words his mother spewed at me alone. I'd gotten my hopes up when I should've known better. It wasn't like this hadn't happened to me before, but in my heart of hearts, I'd thought Landon was different from my ex. Something in his eyes had made it easy for me to trust him. Or maybe I'd misread him. I definitely did, thinking about how Landon and his family were screwing with my livelihood.

A knock on the driver's side window jarred me from my thoughts. I glanced over, not surprised to see Landon casually leaning against my car, looking sexier than any man had the right to do. Gah, why did he have to look so damn delicious? It wasn't fair to the rest of mankind. I inhaled deeply to steel myself against the swarm of butterflies attacking my stomach lining and pressed the button to open my window.

"Yes, can I help you?" I asked, with a little more attitude than I felt, and if the fake censure in my voice affected him even a little, Landon didn't show.

"Has anyone ever told you you're sexy as hell when you're mad?" His lips curled to the side in a sexy smirk. "Probably not. You once told me most dudes are intimidated by you, remember?"

Of course, I remembered, but Landon remembering irritated the hell out of me. I wanted nothing more than to wipe the smirk off his handsome face. Unbuckling my seatbelt, I pushed the door opened, missing Landon by a scant inch, and stepped out the car. "What do you want, Landon?"

Side-stepping Landon, I walked over to the passenger side and grabbed my purse off the seat, but when I spun around, Landon was standing right there. He braced his hands on either side of me, caging me between his hard body and the car. His eyes darkened and slowly slid over my body, heating my skin like a soft caress wherever they landed. The corners of his mouth stretched higher into a full-blown smile.

"You, Gianna, I want you. But since you're playing hard-to-get, I'll relent. However," he stepped closer, eliminating the little space left between us. "You should know I'll give you whatever you want, Gigi, all you have to do is ask nicely."

The slight huskiness of his voice, the heat radiating from his body, the heady mixture of bergamot, spices, and a hint of something naturally him, and his lust-filled gaze all worked in tandem to lower my inhibitions, destroy my resolve. But I refused to give in. Instead of responding, I pushed against the solid wall of his chest until Landon stepped back, dropping both of his arms by his side. I rounded the back of the car, popped the trunk, and grabbed my suitcases.

"I'll get those. Go ahead inside. Your room is upstairs, first door on the left."

I didn't want to argue with Landon or tell him I knew where my room was located since my best friend, Ava, owned the cabin, so I went inside. I needed to put as much space between us as possible. For a brief moment, I almost let my defenses down. Almost.

CHAPTER FOUR

Landon

I watched, hypnotized by the sway of her hips, as Gianna slung her purse strap over her shoulder, grabbed two plastic bags off the backseat, and headed inside the cabin. Once she disappeared, closing the door behind her, I leaned against the car, expelling a breath I hadn't realized I'd been holding. I had no idea how I would make it through this experience. Truth be told, I didn't know if I should be thanking whoever made the sleeping arrangements by sending them a gift basket or cursing them the hell out for torturing me in the most inhumane way possible. Probably the latter. I doubted I would get a semblance of sleep with Gianna's room near mine.

Maybe the universe saw sleepless nights as a form of payback for me hurting Gianna—and her business—by taking over AWA-Dixon. And while she would never admit as such to me—or even herself—I knew I had. The look

Gianna had given me after the smoke cleared had been a mixture of embarrassment and resentment, tinged with a hint of disappointment. Out of the three, knowing I'd disappointed Gianna stung the most.

I was a coward.

Not standing up to my mother had been the catalyst behind this one-sided rivalry Gianna had going on with A Wilson Affair. With me. Call me weird, but while I could do without the petty actions and the bickering between Gianna and I, I'd grown to appreciate and enjoy our back and forth since I interpreted her disdain and resentment towards me as evidence that she cared. Why else would someone continue to hold a grudge for so long, right?

More than anything, I wanted to recapture what Gianna and I had shared the night we met. It had been so easy to talk to Gianna about anything and everything—the weather, the current political climate, expressed outrage over the deaths of unarmed African Americans by the police, our favorite movies, televisions shows, books, and music. We'd even shared the same sentiments concerning protecting the Go-go music culture in DC and not allowing it to be muted after neighbors complained of an establishment playing the music loud during the day. As she spoke about her upbringing, her overbearing father, the expectations she had being the only child of two doctors, I stood enthralled by this amazing woman. And as she listened to me describe my life as a photographer and share the tales from the "road," seeing the wonderment in her beautiful brown eyes, I connected with her on a level I'd never thought I would achieve.

I closed the trunk of the car, grabbed the handles of Gianna's suitcases, and followed the stone path to the front door of the cabin. Once inside, my senses were immediately assaulted by the mouth-watering aroma of the food

I'd purchased from The Sizzling Griddle, along with an unmistakable scent I knew belonged to Gianna. Sweet, alluring, a flavor all her own that beckoned me to follow its trail, across the open concept main floor to the kitchen where she stood next to the sink, peering out of the window into the darkness. Instead of going to her like I so desperately wanted, I climbed the steps to the second floor, deposited Gianna's suitcases inside her room, and headed toward the bedroom I would occupy for the next ten days.

I'd half expected us to be slumming it up in a rinky-dink, tiny house looking box with an outhouse for the bath-room when Janet mentioned the word "cabin". However, the two-story, three-bedroom, three-and-a-half-bathroom structure I'd arrived at this afternoon was nothing like I'd imagined. Polished hardwood floors decorated with thick, plush area rugs and floor-to-ceiling windows allowed natural light to fill the entire space and provided unob-structed views of the mountains in the distance. Contem-porary furnishings provided an inviting ambiance, while a mixture of vibrant paintings and candid shots of a family adorned the walls giving the space a homely feel.

Claiming one of the leather reclining chairs in the corner of the room, I closed my eyes, allowing my mind to wander all its own. From my family and the beautiful woman downstairs who I couldn't seem to get off my mind no matter how many times I'd told myself to let it go, to the career I missed more than anything, and to the one I was trying so hard to navigate. My thoughts were every-where and nowhere at the same time.

"Landon?"

The sound of a feminine voice calling my name, followed by a heavy knock on the bedroom door, forced me to open my eyes. I crossed the room and opened the door, fully expecting to see Gianna on the other side, but was shocked to find Janet pacing back and forth, with one cell phone to her ear and texting on another.

"Evening, Landon," Janet greeted, pulling the phone from her ear, and slipping it in the back pocket of her jeans. "Sorry I wasn't here when you arrived, but I was handling business in Manhattan and got to Maryland less than an hour ago."

"No problem. Thanks for making sure the cabin was ready for my arrival." Last night, during dinner, Janet told Gianna and I not to expect her until after seven because she had some meetings to attend. However, she'd ensured us the property management company assigned to care for the cabin would leave the keys as well as written instructions in a safe spot for us.

"You're welcome. I'm glad your transition here went smoothly." Janet hooked a thumb over her shoulder and motioned towards the steps. "We need you downstairs to go over some rules and give you and Gianna some information about the house and how filming will go. Please bring all of your personal electronics and meet me in the den."

"Got it." Once Janet left, I grabbed both of my items and headed downstairs, but stopped dead in my tracks at the hushed whispers coming from the living room.

"Ava," a voice I instantly recognized as Gianna's said. "Did you know?"

"Know what? About the wedding here or you being required to stay here while planning?"

"As messed up as it is that you knew the location of the wedding, and the fact they wanted to hire me and didn't say anything, that's not why I'm pissed at you, and from that funky ass smirk you're trying hard to keep at bay, I'm guessing you knew I would have to stay here with him."

"Hmmm... It must've slipped my mind."

"Slipped your mind? Do you seriously expect me to believe you suddenly developed a case of amnesia?"

I envisioned Gianna pacing back and forth, hands on her hips, nostrils flaring, and smoke shooting from her ears like a cartoon character.

A soft laugh filled the air. "Do you even hear yourself, Gi? I know you don't because if you did, you'd realize how crazy you sound right now. I had to sign a NDA just like you, and you're mad because you're staying in the same room you've stayed in every summer since we were kids."

Since kids? This meant when I'd given Gianna directions on where to find her room, she'd not only known where it was, but she'd spent time here before and hadn't said anything. I shook my head with a smile. Leave it to Gianna to skimp on the details.

"Look, Gianna, whatever happened between you and him, you gotta let it go because this—you insinuating I set you up—is insane."

I couldn't hear Gianna's response. So, I descended the stairs, startling both women. I could see the questions swimming in Gianna's eyes. "Evening, ladies." I walked over to where Gianna and Ava stood and extended my hand to Ava. "Hi, I'm Landon Wilson."

Ava's eyes widened and her lips curved into a knowing smile as she accepted my proffered hand. "It's finally nice to meet you, Landon. I've heard a lot about you. I'm Ava."

"Nice to meet you, Ava." I divided a glance between Ava and Gianna, my gaze lingered on Gianna. "Whatever Gianna has told you, don't believe her," I joked, hoping to relieve some of the awkwardness. "She won't allow me to show her my good side."

"Don't take it personally, Landon." Ava leaned forward and cupped a hand to her mouth. "I've known Gianna since we were four-years-old. Showing emotion means she cares."

Gianna rolled her eyes at me, turned towards Ava. "Showing emotion means nothing."

I smirked at that reply.

Hours later, as I laid in bed, I couldn't help but smile. Ava's words of wisdom replayed in my head on a loop, along with the look in Gianna's eyes—a mixture of defiance, confusion, and fear, like maybe her friend had hipped me to something she'd wished I didn't know. I didn't know how, but I planned to make Gianna see there was more to me than the man she'd met, the man who'd walked away and left her to deal with Josephine Wilson. I had ten days to get it done because who knew when—or if—I would have another chance like this again.

CHAPTER FIVE

Gianna

Closing my eyes, I pinched the bridge of my nose and took what was supposed to be a calming breath. Only it didn't help alleviate the tension settling in my shoulders. It didn't calm or mellow me out, not even a little bit. The longer I listened to the smooth jazz rendition of "Back Dat Ass Up" by Juvenile, the more irritated I became. What type of florist would use this song for their hold music? I knew the answer even before I thought of the question but refused to say it. I wouldn't recommend a vendor like this to my clients. I had no idea why Jonquis and Azura chose this florist, but this ratchet ass on-hold music was strike two against them, unprecedented since we'd only been planning the wedding for less than seventy-two hours. Strike one happened when an employee of the shop promised an all-white bouquet of Cabbage roses to Azura. The issue? They only bloomed in the spring and early summer and were currently out of season for this late autumn wedding.

"Still on hold?" Landon asked, entering the dining room.

I glanced from the notepad I'd idly been doodling on. I wouldn't pretend I didn't want to tell Landon to choke on a fat one or that I wasn't wishing an imaginary hole would appear for him to fall into. But for now, we were co-workers, and planning this wedding was a team effort. Still, Landon and his presence had plucked my nerves since my arrival. For the most part, our working relationship was going smoothly. We'd had a couple of small hiccups such as celebrities not responding to the RSVPs as directed, broken items we'd received via the mail, lost packages, and other items, but we'd worked through them together. However, our personal relationship—me hating him—was another story.

Factoring in the smart comments he constantly made, him purposely talking, laughing, or playing music loud in the middle of the night, hogging the only television in the house, and generally being an asshole? Living with Landon felt more like having the college roommate from hell. Then again, I did make it a tad bit easy for him to practically take over my childhood hangout by confining myself to my room when we weren't working. I was still a little peeved at him for showing up while Ava and I were talking about him. I was pretty sure he'd heard most, if not all, of the conversation, but he hadn't alluded to such.

I nodded. "Yeah and it's irritating me. This hold music ain't helping." I tapped the screen, placing the phone on speaker.

Landon walked closer, the smell of his body's natural scent and the cologne he wore, wafted to my nose. His eyebrow furrowed as he bobbed his head to the beat of the song. Finally, after a few seconds, Landon's eyes widened in recognition. "Who the hell uses a smooth jazz version 'Tip Drill' as their hold music?"

Unable to stop myself, I burst out laughing. "This company. I've been on hold for the past fifteen minutes, and so far, I've heard 'Thong Song,' 'Back Dat Ass Up,' and now 'Tip Drill.' I don't know who selected the hold music, or why, but this is not it."

"Not at all," Landon chuckled.

He walked over to the fridge, grabbed a bottle of water, and leaned against the counter; his gaze focused on me. All traces of amusement evaporated from his face and it now held an inscrutable expression. Yet, for some inexplicable reason, I could decipher the look in his eyes. I knew what Landon thought, what he'd wanted to say, even before he could open his mouth and speak it into existence.

And I only had myself to blame.

I hadn't meant to open a can of worms the night that Landon and I had met with Janet at Wolf Creek Inn, but I had when I'd mentioned what happened between us ten months ago. It was an overdue conversation that Landon had tried to start several times over the past three days, but I didn't want to discuss it. Not now. Not ever. Because telling Landon how I felt watching him walk away as I stood there listening to his mother systematically break me by calling out every one of my insecurities like she'd spent time talking to my father and had taken notes, would have forced me to relive the pain once again.

I didn't want to dredge up memories of the gut-wrenching pain I'd suffered at the hands of my first love. It had been almost a decade since the night we'd broken up, and while it hadn't been easy, I'd finally gotten over him. But the emotional scars I still carried served as a reminder of what happened when I let my guard down and left my heart unattended.

I didn't want to deal with any of this right now. Where was a miracle when I needed it?

"Gianna, I…"

Thankfully, I got my answer. Someone in heaven must've put in a good word to the Big Man for me, or God himself saw the tears clouding my vision though I refused to let them fall and took pity on me. The hold music abruptly cut off and a male voice filled the air.

"Thank you for holding, this is Marley. How can I help you?"

"Hi, Marley. My name is Gianna Johnson, the owner of Splendid Soirees." I removed the phone off speakerphone. "I received an email from your business asking me to call immediately concerning order number…" I flipped through the notepad for the order number I'd scribbled down and began to read it to the man when the hairs on the back of my neck stood on end.

I glanced over to find Landon watching me. The intense scrutiny had me shifting in my seat. He folded his arms over his broad chest, cocked his head to the side – obviously not pleased by the interruption – and expelled a breath. Landon grabbed the bottle of water he'd placed beside him and pushed off the counter, walking away. His walk should've been considered illegal. The way he stalked was almost deadly and predatorial.

He moved towards me and leaned in, bracing both his hands on the sides of me, and whispered, "This isn't over, Gianna." The warmth of his breath fanned my cheek, causing an explosion of sensations to course through my veins. "You keep giving me the runaround, but guess what, sweetheart? It's just you and me here for the next week. We'll talk a lot sooner than later."

As Landon left the dining area for the den, I couldn't help but remind myself how it could all be so simple if I'd allowed him to say his peace and finally spoke the truth on my heart. But I couldn't because the thought of rejection in addition to his family trying to destroy my business—my legacy—made it hard. He might've thought we would sit and talk about what had happened between us, but not if I had any say so.

CHAPTER SIX

Landon

One thing I hated more than anything was being asked to do something at the last minute. Granted, I was co-planning a wedding scheduled to take place in five days, but Azura and Jonquis were quickly become more than just the King and Queen of R&B and Hip-Hop. I'd secretly started calling them the King and Queen of Procrastination since they'd waited until the very last minute to make changes or do anything that Gianna and I had requested of them. Today had been no different.

Earlier, as we gave the couple updates on the wedding planning process, Azura and Jonquis sprung another task on Gianna and me. We were now in charge of selecting the wine, champagne, and the signature drinks for both receptions. The smaller one would take place directly after the wedding in a tent in the spacious backyard of the cabin for the, now, eighty people invited. The second reception would happen later that evening at Wolf Lodge Inn with more than three-hundred people.

A part of me couldn't wait until this event was over. Not because of the hard work going into it, but because earlier during the video conference I'd barely recognized myself. As I sat there watching Jonquis flash his trademark billion-watt smile, one I'd seen grown women cry and fight over, my eyes kept sliding to Gianna to gauge her reaction. Yes, I was Drake'n...hard. In my feelings over the possibility of Gianna being one of the millions of women ready to risk it all for even the briefest moment with him. Jonquis, by most standards, would be considered attractive. Tall, light-skinned pretty boy with curly hair, light golden-brown eyes, and tattoos covering his arms looking like a page out of an adult coloring book. I wasn't hating or anything, but I damn sure hadn't wanted to sit there and watch the woman I wanted fangirling over a dude who could pass for a member of DeBarge.

I laughed at the comparison now, as I slipped on a tank top, a pair of basketball shorts, and my Nike slides, preparing myself to head downstairs for the tasting. I'd lied to Gianna earlier, telling her I had a headache and needed to take a nap. But the truth was I didn't want Gianna to be afraid of me or hate me so much she would rather stay cooped up in her room than explore the cabin she'd been visiting since childhood. Of course, I wanted to talk to her about what had happened between us and try to get a better understanding where we could co-exist as planners —at least for the two remaining months I would be in charge of AWA-Dixon. I guess, for now, I would wait for her to bring up the topic.

Leaving the room, I headed downstairs. "Thanks for waking me…" the words died on my lips as my foot landed on the last step. My eyes scanned the living room, taking in its transformation to a romantic scene straight from a movie. Dim lighting set the mood, with the help of candles sporadically placed throughout the room. The flames of the fireplace crackled in harmony with the soft music piping through hidden speakers. The inviting furniture had been replaced with a circular table set for two. I walked further into the living room, finding Gianna standing next to a table full of different desserts. "Damn, Gigi. I went to sleep thinking you hated me and wake up to you trying to seduce me; talk about a full one-eighty."

"Don't flatter your damn self, I didn't do—" she turned and waved a hand towards the table, "—this. Gianna held up a card in her hands. "Apparently, Jonquis and Azura want to thank us for all we've done."

"Sure, sweetheart, blame it on them. I won't tell anyone." I stopped next to Gianna, grabbed a chocolate-covered strawberry and took a bite. "Now, are you ready to do this because I've been waiting all day." I pulled out Gianna's chair, sat across from her, and after watching the video that the mixologist had prepared for us, we began the tasting.

"I don't like this one," Gianna frowned, her words a little slurred. She pushed the glass of Sangiovese to the side.

If Gianna hadn't been tipsy after we'd selected two signature drinks—one made with Hennessy and the other with white rum—I knew when we started sampling the champagne and wine, she'd be gone. And I was right. She was done. Gianna had casually mentioned not being a big drinker a couple of times, so I wasn't surprised by the random giggling, slurred words, and the glossiness of her doe-shaped eyes.

"Lannndddooonnn," Gianna half-sung, half whined.

I covered my mouth with a napkin to keep from laughing. "Yes, beautiful."

Instead of responding, Gianna gasped. Her expression, filled with a playfulness I'd enjoyed seeing after those first couple of drinks, changed into one of stone. She stood, shaking her head as she walked over to the dessert table. "Don't call me beautiful." I opened my mouth to ask about the sudden change in her demeanor, but Gianna held up a hand. "Because we both know it's a lie. Everything you've ever said to me, especially the night we met, has been nothing more than a game to you."

"What are you talking about?" I asked, leaping from my chair to follow Gianna. "I've never lied to you."

Gianna let out a bitter laugh, the ugliness of its sound, surprising me. "You know what, forget it. It doesn't even matter because nothing you say tonight changes anything. It doesn't erase anything your mother said, and it damn sure won't save Splendid Soirees since you and your horrible ass mother are both hellbent on destroying my legacy."

CHAPTER SEVEN

Gianna

As soon as the words left my mouth, I'd wanted to snatch them back. I'd held ‧onto this information since A Wilson Affair came to the area. The words caused a searing pain to grip my body the moment I spoke them. Knowing something that I had poured my blood, sweat, and tears into was being systematically dismantled by Landon and his mother infuriated me more than the confusion written on his handsome face and my attraction to him.

I didn't care about being drunk as hell. The more I stood face-to-face with Landon, in a room decorated for a night of seduction with its soft lighting, baby-making music, and whole romantic ambiance, the more I wanted to go upside his head with one of these bottles of ridiculously expensive wine. But my girls taught me better than to waste good liquor. Hell, being friends with Ava and Delaney, I knew better than to waste the cheap stuff too.

Besides, I didn't want to go to jail, and assaulting Landon would only get me a one-way trip in the back of a police cruiser to a waiting cell. Not only would it be bad for my business, but my parents would disown me. With Delaney's twin brother being a cop, it would get back to her, and I'd would have to hear her mouth as well.

"Gianna, I have no idea what you're talking about. How did I destroy your business? I thought Splendid Soirees was doing well. You said so yourself."

"We were…I mean, we are no thanks to you and your mother." There were about a hundred other names I wanted to refer to Josephine Wilson as and none of them included "Child of God." The woman was vile. Disgusting. A bitter old hag who sucked the happiness from people, like a Dementor from the Harry Potter movies. But she was also an elder and one thing my parents had drilled into my head non-stop was to respect my elders. It had been the only thing that saved her snooty ass from catching a curse out and these hands the night we'd met.

"But what did we do?" Landon asked, tossing his hands up in frustration. "You've yet to say. All you've done was hurl accusations and blame me for something I know nothing about."

I laughed, though I found nothing about the situation or this conversation remotely funny. "You're one helluva actor, Landon. A whole lot better than my ex-boyfriend. Two assholes who would say and do anything to get into the drawers. The only difference is while you were too much of a coward to stick around to listen to your mother tell me I would never be good enough for you because I was 'the help', Anthony stayed right there, by his parents' side, agreeing with his mother when she told me I would never get their blessing to marry their son because my only claim to fame was being a disappointment to my parents.

He'd looked me dead in my eyes when his father suggested he keep me as his mistress since everyone knew girls like me—ghetto hoodrats—were freaks. He'd stood right beside me as he confirmed his father's suspicions, detailing our sexual encounters, and how he'd been my first lover, as I fought back tears. Then, he called a pretty little high saditty chick over and introduced her as his fiancée." I wasn't surprised at the silence following my admission. What could Landon say to separate himself from being compared to a man like Anthony?

Nothing. Abso-fucking-lutely nothing.

"Gianna, I'm sorry you experienced that. Dude's a straight-up punk bitch who needs his ass handed to him, but—" he shook his head, touching a hand to his chest. "I would never. You know me, Gianna. I respect you. Yeah, I might do things to rile you up, but pissing you off is the only way I can get you to talk to me and respond to me."

"I don't know you," I countered, moving to the other side of the room. I needed to get as far away from Landon as possible. I'd had trouble focusing all night because of his closeness and the unique aromas I'd come to associate with only him. Add the wines, champagnes, and the liquor? My current state of inebriation made this a recipe for disaster. "We talked, we had a lot of things in common, hell, we may have even made a connection, but it didn't mean a damn thing to you when you decided to head the AWA-Dixon office after your mother threatened to destroy Splendid Soirees when Laney and I decided not to sell to her."

The war of emotions raging inside of Landon marred the flawless features of his face. The shock and disbelief of my words only lasting mere seconds before his eyes flashed with anger. "Are you serious?" he shouted.

I knew he'd asked the question not expecting an

answer, but I gave him one anyway. "Yes." Maybe it was my need to break through the wall of silence filling the room, or maybe a part of me needed to confirm the severity of the situation out loud—to myself and to Landon. Whatever the reason, doing so failed to alleviate the weight that rested on my shoulders and seemed to echo within the space between us.

"So you hate me because of what my mother did?" Landon crossed the room, stopping in front of me. He reached out, his hands lingering near my cheek, before he thought better of it and shoved them into his pockets. "Gianna, you have to believe me, I knew nothing about my mother's offer to buy your company or the threats she made."

The raw emotion in his voice, the pleading in his eyes, and something I could only attribute to naivete—since I'd always wanted to see the good in a person even if they'd shown me otherwise—caused me to believe Landon wholeheartedly. I quickly remembered what being naïve had once gotten me and wouldn't allow myself to let this go so easily.

"I-I don't know. I have no idea what to think right now." I hated how weak and vulnerable my voice sounded to my own ears. Memories came rushing back with the force of a category five hurricane. All the emotions: the embarrassment, anger, and resentment, made me pissed all over again. "You may have not known about your mother's offer to buy Splendid Soirees, but it's no coincidence you opened the AWA-Dixon office two weeks after we met, Landon. If memory serves me correctly, you were supposed to be on location, so what happened? Why didn't you go to Mexico?"

I observed Landon carefully, searching for even the slightest hint of nervousness in his expression. Anything to alert me to the lie I wanted to believe he'd told. But the longer I stared him, watching the flicker of the flames from the candles dance along his skin, the easier it became to identify his expression, although his eyes were trained on the floor, disappointment.

"I didn't go to Mexico because my parents—namely, my mother—convinced my grandmother to cut me off." Finally, he glanced at me, the remorse in his gaze stole the breath from my lungs. I'd never seen this man before. Sure, he looked and sounded like Landon, but gone was the arrogance I'd grown used to from his demeanor. He appeared vulnerable and unsure of himself?

"And the only way I could regain access to my trust fund was to agree to run the AWA-Dixon office for a year and make it succeed."

I didn't know what I'd expected to come from Landon's mouth, but I damn sure wasn't expecting that.

CHAPTER EIGHT

Landon

There, I'd said it. I'd told Gianna, the woman whose opinion of me I valued more than my parents, I'd been forced to quit the career I'd fallen in love with over two decades ago when my grandfather gifted me my first camera. It had been a Polaroid, but there'd been something empowering in capturing moments in time and freezing them forever. But I gave it up without much of a fight. What hurt the most about my decision to walk away from my first love was how cheap it made me feel, knowing I'd thrown away my dream for money.

I hated to admit I was a sellout out loud. Seeing the shock written on Gianna's face didn't make me feel any better, but after she'd dropped a bomb on me, I'd needed Gianna to understand I wasn't involved in whatever dumb shit my mother had been plotting.

The more Gianna's words played on a loop in my head, the more it made sense. My mother had always been the kind of woman who stopped at nothing to get what she wanted. The night of the anniversary party—and days leading up to it—she'd been upset that my godparents Eleanor and Kendrick Davenport had decided to hire an outsider to plan their event, especially since my mother and Eleanor had been best friends and roommates since college.

"Your parents forced you to quit your job as a photographer? Why?"

"The same reason you believe you're a disappointment to your parents," I answered with a shrug. "Before becoming a photographer, I'd worked as an accountant at my father's firm with my brother. I never enjoyed it but did so because I thought it would make them proud of me. Only—"

"They continued to criticize you," Gianna finished for me.

I nodded. "Soon, I grew tired of it. If I couldn't make my parents happy working where they'd wanted me to, going to the schools they'd chosen for me, living where they'd decided, I would do what I wanted to do regardless of what they thought of me. When I quit the firm, they were pissed, but becoming a photographer sent them through the roof. The first few years of my photography career, I'd had the support of my grandfather as well as the nest egg I'd saved. But back in January, my grandfather passed away."

I swallowed the lump in my throat and closed my eyes to steel myself against the onslaught of sadness threatening to consume me. "My father—who'd been his accountant— discovered the secret trust my granddad set up for me and told my mother. They both hated the idea of me being a photographer and were livid to discover my granddad had funded my career choice. They went to my grandmother and talked her into freezing the trust since he'd never attached my name to the account to keep it hidden."

"Wow, Landon. I'm so sorry your parents are insufferable jackasses, especially your mother." She clapped a hand over her mouth. "My bad, I shouldn't be talking about your parents."

"Nah, you're good," I chuckled. "My parents are assholes. They lived most of their marriage together being miserable, divorced, married other people—my mom is on her third marriage—and because they haven't found happiness, they're determined to make sure no one else is happy."

"Damn shame you had to give up your dream career for what belonged to you, Landon," her cute little nose wrinkled as she frowned. "You let them win. You're not happy being a planner."

"It's partially true. I was happier as a photographer, but I've learned to like being an event planner. As much as I wanna quit now, and say to hell with it, it's a Catch 22. Quitting would mean my parents were right, that I'd had an easy life because of my family's name. But I don't want you to lose Splendid Soirees, Gianna." I groaned, unsure of what to do.

Gianna sighed. "Landon, you can't quit. I won't let you, not for me, not because you think it's right. Call me petty, but I want you to prove your parents wrong. Don't walk away from AWA-Dixon until your year is over."

Closing the gap between us, my thumb caressed the soft, supple skin of her cheek. To think, my mother had all but tried to break this incredibly beautiful, strong, intelligent woman. Her ex-boyfriend almost succeeded in breaking her spirit. Even her parents, the man and woman who were supposed to love and protect her had tried to clip her wings, preventing this butterfly from taking flight. But staring into her big brown eyes, I knew they'd all failed.

"Are you sure?"

Smiling, Gianna nodded. "Positive."

Gianna was special. I'd known this the moment we'd locked eyes ten months ago. I'd felt this magnetic pull to her, and although I'd told myself to look away, I hadn't been able to. She'd drawn me in like a moth to a flame, and I could admit, at the time, it had unnerved me. I'd never met a woman who'd had me thinking about the future. Images of what could be—what would be—had flashed through my head like a dream sequence in a movie, with Gianna starring as my leading lady.

I'd dated, but nothing serious enough to make me want to trade in my Downtown DC condo for a single-family house in the suburbs or my 2020 Audi R8 Coupe – which sat two – for a family-sized SUV. Until Gianna. If love at first sight was real, I'd fallen for Gianna in an instant, hence me going the extra length to get under her skin. But I couldn't tell her this without possibly scaring her the hell off.

So, instead, I said, "I'm sorry for the part I played in my mother's scheme and how your business has suffered because of her. It was never my intention, Gianna."

"Thanks, Landon," Gianna shrugged. "But you had no idea what she was doing, so I can't hold her actions against you. I'm sorry I blamed you. I allowed my insecurities and the pain of my past to cloud my judgment. Yeah, you're annoying as hell, but I knew better than to believe you were vindictive."

"Damn, annoying, though?" I laughed. My chest swelled with pride when Gianna joined in on the laughter.

Once it subsided, I continued, "I can also see why you compared me to ol' dude. But not everything he did," I added quickly. "Your ex was foul. Still, even if I didn't take up for you, I should've stopped my mother from disrespecting you. I regret not doing so, Gianna. Because we could've already been together."

Gianna pursed her lips together, though the corners twitched with the makings of a smile. "Oh, really? What makes you think I wanna get with you?"

"Who wouldn't want to be with me?" I jumped back to dodge the jab she threw at me. I grabbed her, pulling her back into my arms, her body fitting so perfectly against mine. Holding her close, it was almost like she belonged there. Like two pieces connecting to finish a 1000-piece puzzle. "But in all seriousness, things could've turned out differently."

"Maybe, but due to the freezing of your trust, you still would've been forced to work for your family's business. We would've still ended up here."

"Maybe. I can't control the past, but I can put some things in motion to set up my future." I cupped her face in my hands, lowering my lips until they hovered inches from hers.

"Like what?" Gianna asked, her voice barely above a whisper.

"Like kissing you how I've wanted to do since meeting you. Then, once we get this wedding out the way, going to dinner like we'd planned."

Standing on her tiptoes, Gianna wrapped her arms around my neck and pressed her body against the growing hardness of my erection. "What else?"

"I can show you better than I can tell you." I scooped Gianna up off the floor, into my arms, and carried her upstairs, laughing at her squeals of delight. I had no idea what the future held for us or what would even happen once we finished this event, but I was determined to keep Gianna in my life and in my arms for as long as she would have me. Preferably forever.

THE END

ACKNOWLEDGMENTS

First and foremost, to my Lord and Savior. I'm grateful for this gift of writing you've blessed me with. Thank you for all you've done and have yet to do in my life.

To my little big sister, Saronda. You are the sunshine of my life. Thank you, for EVERYTHING. We got this!!

To my family and friends who have supported me and this dream especially Kyshana, Niecy, Brook, Carolyn, and Ms. Sheryl. Thank you for your constant support, encouragement, and more importantly, your love.

To Leslie, Sheryl, Anita, Angela, and Sherelle. Thank you for believing in me enough to give me this chance. Words fail to describe how grateful I am for you, your support, and mentoring. Thank you!

ABOUT KIMMIE FERRELL

Born and raised in Washington, DC, Kimmie has enjoyed reading romance novels since the age of thirteen when she was gifted an enormous box of Harlequin and Silhouette novels from her late mother.

Kimmie crafts sensual and sweet contemporary romance stories featuring relatable characters dealing with real-world scenarios in the pursuit for the often-thought-as-elusive happily ever after.

For more information, visit her website at www.authorkimmieferrell.com

 facebook.com/AuthorKimmieFerrell
 twitter.com/KimmieFerrell
 instagram.com/kimmieferrell

UBER INTENTIONS

CANDICE JOHNSON

Laken's debut novel is poised to blow up every book list. But author Knight's poisonous pen - and plagiarism lawsuit - threatens her potential best-selling title. Not only are they former secret friends with benefits, but they're essentially telling the same story. Will Knight and Laken remain enemies? Or will they reconcile… via Uber?

To my husband, "Hershey." Thank you for your love, and inspiring me to keep my pen moving.

CHAPTER ONE

Groping for Acquittal

Laken

"Do you always kiss strangers like this?" His labored breath traced the question across my tingling neck.

"Only strangers who straddle me in the back of an Uber," I replied before trapping my bottom lip between my teeth.

We stopped talking abruptly; the clothes we'd frantically ripped off each other commandeered the conversation, the sounds of our lips locking providing the soundtrack to this excursion no one who knew me would ever believe. Here I was - a shy, hapless, hopeless romantic, terrified of my own shadow, beating the brakes off an '02 Ford Taurus with a scrumptious man whose name I didn't even know, not giving a flip about my religious upbringing, my nosy girlfriends' opinions, or what this man would think of me after my pent-up desires drove him to the brink of sensual insanity. He was too fine for me to care about repercussions.

It was hot.

It was unreal.

And I was proud.

My girls would call me a skank — should I ever confess, and that's exactly what I would be. I'd be a skank. A skank who was finally satisfied…just the freaky way I desired.

The only thing that kept me from reaching over to scrape the smug grin from Knight Bradley's face with the heel of my stiletto was the death grip my lawyer had on my arm as the mediator read the passage from my unreleased novel, *Uber Intentions*, aloud. Either I was having hot flashes, or the air conditioning in the dank conference room at the law firm of Madison and Glover had gone out. Either way, I was ten ticks past pissed.

I'd admit in the past, my brother's sexy best friend made me blush more than a few times, but litigation was drastically different than our steamy college trysts. Back then, Derek was oblivious to the peep shows Knight and I would perform whenever he was passed out drunk in the compact apartment they shared. Today, we tossed aside childish secrets in favor of grown folks business. This mediation concerned me more than making sure my legs were shaved and we had enough condoms to last the duration of our impromptu hook-ups. Dude was attacking my intellectual property on top of my integrity…and when the legalities were over, I planned to choke Knight like a chicken.

"After reading a portion of Miss Cross's manuscript and reviewing my client's published work, I believe everyone can agree that *Uber Intentions* bears a striking resemblance to Mr. Bradley's masterpiece, *Consummating the Uber*. Therefore, we are requesting publication of Miss Cross's book cease immediately."

I'd moseyed into this farce, accused of plagiarizing my benefit-less buddy's trashy book, determined I wouldn't act a donkey or a cliché.

My prayer was vehemently denied.

"Knight Bradley's *masterpiece* smells a lot like feces to me." I drove my fist into the metal desk, wishing my opponent's face was underneath it. The sharp pain didn't give me time to regret the knee-jerk response, as rage spilled from my mouth. "Who would want to steal something so stupid? That street drivel Knight wrote is nothing like *Uber Intentions*. This fool should be thanking me for raising his intellect past *Pootie Tang*."

"So you admit my client's work has at the very least influenced your book?" Knight's snooty attorney eyed me over the small round frames which did nothing to compliment her narrow face. The drably dressed woman paced the front of the room, taupe kitten heels drumming against the tile as if she was a church usher. Even the gap separating her front teeth was arrogant.

"I admit your client is a moron who lifts his plots and all their holes from reality television." I flipped my loose hair over my shoulders, upset that I spent hours straightening it to sit on a throne of accusations like a Salem witch, with my former lover sadistically spearheading the hunt. My edges were reverting back as I inched closer to clenching a restraining order on top of an injunction.

"First of all, I write urban novels, Laken Cross. Urban. Don't knock my art because you're struggling." Knight's gorgeous almond eyes narrowed until I could barely make out the stunning hazel in his peepers. The way he enunciated my full name like a stranger made me want to puke. You didn't speak to a woman whose panties had been in your mouth that way.

"Call my books stupid all you want—my royalties make me a genius," he spat.

…couldn't argue with that. Dang.

"Your Honor, I would like to read a passage from Mr. Bradley's novel for a bit of clarity." My lawyer, Johnston, eased in with the rebuttal my boggled mind failed to articulate. He slid his hand over mine to keep me calm.

"I see no problem with that, Counselor," the female judge presiding over the case confirmed. "Proceed."

"Very well." Johnston released my hand, flipped through some pages and stood, slowly pacing for dramatic effect. Knowing what was about to be read turned my caramel cheeks bright crimson. I wasn't ready for all my business to be put in the street but exposing myself was the only way to keep Knight and his rock-hard abs from winning an injunction against my literary dreams.

…and ensuring I'd never find myself consuming his chocolate skin again.

"This wasn't the same unassuming angel who picked me up in a red Escort an hour earlier," Johnston narrated. "Before we reached my destination, the mousy female transformed into a ferocious freak, digging her long nails in my bare back, snatching the sides of my 'fro, biting my neck, moaning as I dove deeper into her sea. I served every inch of her willing body my *membership rewards*; her full lips responded in kind with tricks only her virginity thief could have taught her."

The more Johnston recited, the more unamused I was, having bits and pieces of my sordid sexual history - albeit somewhat fictionalized through Knight's twisted pen, thrown in my face. A classic booty breach. He wrote in a few extra curves and added dimples, but the sin-sational, uninhibited heroine of his erotic tale was definitely based on the night the book whore seated across from me, dressed in a t-shirt bearing his arrogant face, became the first man I slept with.

I regretted ever allowing this guy to get close enough to get a whiff.

"My anonymous conquest's long legs clamped around my waist, forcing me to move faster," Johnston quickly read, "I pulled her auburn-streaked hair and obliged her wishes for more. Her cherry flavored gloss provided the perfect blend of sweet with the salt drenching her skin. Her brown eyes weren't as barren as they were when I climbed in her vehicle; the colorful tattoo of a trio of tacos on her left forearm looked ready to eat as she grasped for everything that made me a man."

Knight listened intensely as I tugged the sleeves of my purple turtleneck down, hoping no one would notice his spot-on description of the culinary ink on my arms. His content expression seemed to be reminiscing rather than conjuring up a defense for scandalizing me. If I'd known he was this gutter, I would have dropped the dime to Derek that his best bud was screwing me, so he could kick his fine tail. But since I could actually keep a secret, I had no choice but to feel the burn while the smug grin creeping through Knight's manicured mustache confirmed the ode to my…*talents*. I knew I had put it on him, but dang.

"Your Honor, this is crazy. Everything counsel just read supports my client's position that Miss Cross read *Consummating the Uber*, rearranged a few words and descriptions, then slapped a different title on it. Let's call plagiarism by its name so we can all get home to our families." Knight's nervy lawyer drummed a pen on the metal desk, locking eyes with me. She was judging; I was seething. Knight scooped a glass of water in his hands, sipping like he was enjoying the tea. I had something else he could sip…but it might land me in protective custody.

Johnston flung his hand in front of me, the way mothers did to block their kids from flying through the passenger seat window when mama braked too hard in the car. I slunk in my seat, feeling muzzled.

"Your Honor, contrary to what opposing counsel would have us to believe, Mr. Bradley's own words corroborate what we've been arguing all along – *Consummating the Uber* is the result of pillow talk between two –" Johnston paused to peer at me over his shoulder for approval before blurting, "lovers. Mr. Bradley and Miss Cross are former lovers."

"Hold on now!" Miss magistrate-of-the-court released a joyous squeal like reality show reunion fisticuffs were happening before her gray eyes. I was feeling froggy enough to jump and give her a great show, too. "So you two got something going on?" The woman's head bobbed enthusiastically between us.

Knight responded first, not that I was shocked; he'd never been much of a gentleman. "In the past, Laken and I have...shared expressions," he admitted with a sheepish wink through his luscious lashes. "But nothing more."

"Shared expressions? Who says that?" I yelped. "I got your expressions, jerk. You and I both know I *expressed* the synopsis of *Uber Intentions* while you were in between my legs on Christmas break from Crayton U senior year. So not only are you a panty thief...you're a plot klepto."

Knight choked on the rotisserie crow I served him. The animated face on his t-shirt disintegrated under the cool liquid as it dripped from his parted lips, dumbfounded shock frozen on his handsome face. I hated how even in spite of his evil ways...this man was impeccably scrumptious.

Jerk.

"Is this true?" The judge smoothed a hand over her

sleek bun, before scribbling a few notes on the pad in front of her.

"Well, ummm…" Knight hem-hawed, drying his damp mouth on his sleeve.

"I'll take that as a yes," her honor said. "Counselors, this revelation changes the dynamics of this case. We're going to recess for today and reconvene after I've had the chance to sort this out."

"Yes, Your Honor," both lawyers replied in unison.

"Miss Cross," the judge addressed me before nodding at Knight, snickering, "You're released for today and will be updated on next steps soon." She released a sigh sounding almost like a moan as she scooped both of our books in her hands. "In the meantime…I've got some reading to do, chile."

CHAPTER TWO

All in my Feelings

Knight

Laken was sexier than I remembered.

...even more edible if she would quit scowling like she wanted to sink a machete into my chest.

"My sister's going to gut you like a fish." Derek lowered the brim of his denim cap over his eyes, shielding himself from Laken's death glare. Even though my long body stretched well beyond six feet, I had to admit in spite of how great she looked, the pint-sized filly spitting fire from across the room intimidated me. She was dressed in a plush pink blazer and matching fitted skirt showing off her smooth legs. The front of her wavy hair was pulled into a high ponytail and the rest hung loosely around her shoulders – her homage to Whitley Gilbert for the 90's television show themed party. Her attire was proper and pristine, but her thuggish glare hadn't melted since I arrived at Shrimp 'N Gritz Catering and Event Center to celebrate Derek's engagement. In fact, Laken had barely blinked in the last thirty minutes. I was used to women staring at me…but not while potentially plotting my death.

"You two have to get this mess worked out before the wedding," Derek's amused voice snapped me from my trance. "Java's holding me and my loins accountable for your screw up. My entire body's blue, bro." Dressed in overalls as Overton Wakefield Jones from Living Single, Derek's hands dropped, rubbing a region I didn't care to set eyes on.

"First of all…loins?" One of my eyebrows rose at my buddy's goofy choice of description.

"Man, Java got saved. Again. She made me promise to clean up my vocabulary." Derek grumbled the explanation through chugs of beer. "What I'm saying is, my fiancée hasn't held out on me this long since college."

"Good – if you're born again then you shouldn't be fornicating anyway, right?" I hollered my question over "It Takes Two" by Rob Base blaring through the hall's speakers. Party people were boogieing on the dance floor, bombarding the buffet tables and posing for pictures in front of a gigantic backdrop with "Derek & Java: 2+2 = FOREVER" brightly painted in graffiti. In spite of the festive atmosphere, Laken's pissy vibes continued shaking me, so I popped on my Dwayne Wayne flip shades to make myself invisible. Even with the dark barrier between us, Laken remained motionless, staring like she was about to ambush me with a machete and a hockey mask, but it wasn't Halloween.

I found the nerve to speak. "It's been weeks since my

case was dismissed. I lost. Laken should be happy and over it by now."

Derek bolted straight up in the leather upholstered chair, confusion clouding his round face. "Over it? Have you met my sister? She collects grudges – along with male body parts that rhyme with walls – and nails them to the wall."

The thought of angry bird Laken coming anywhere near pertinent parts of my anatomy made me cringe. I lowered my head and pulled my jacket closed, trying not to spy on Laken and Java, huddled by the cash bar. I felt a thousand curse words attached to my name behind their angry faces

I knew I should've skipped this shindig.

"Look at them. Probably over there talking about me," I observed.

"You always think women are talking about you, Knight." Derek snatched his cap off and massaged his bald head. "Just because you're bearded and pretty doesn't mean every woman wants you, sucka."

As if on cue, a few sistas strolled by our table, inserting some extra oomph in their wiggles and sly winks – flirting in spite of knowing good and well at least one of us was already spoken for. "Women love me," I chuckled. "But that's not my point. I'm telling you, Laken has something up her sleeve. I smell venom all the way over here."

"Listen – I could care less what's going on between y'all, even though you could have given a brother the head's up you were banging my sister a long time ago."

"Don't make it sound so bad, Derek," I interrupted with my hand raised like a stop sign. "Besides, you would have tried to kill me if I said something and you know it."

"Doesn't matter now, Knight. You and Laken are grown. Grown-grown. So be grown enough to apologize and let me get married in peace." Derek checked me before acknowledging more attractive passers-by. I guess the excessive amount of estrogen hovering around our table was a bit much, because Java – in her Khadijah James get-up, plopped in Derek's lap before I blinked.

"Hey, babe." Java planted a sloppy wet one on Derek, leaving his dark lips stained red. She hugged his neck hard and waved to the ladies who'd been flirting, almost like she was throwing a gang sign. "Knight," she addressed me dryly.

"Java." I nodded, suddenly finding the cold plate of hot wings in front of me appealing.

"You still living vicariously in my girl's lady parts through your insipid books?"

…I knew they had been conspiring.

I mustered up as much decorum as I could before answering, "Your girl needs to pull her head out of her delusional tail and admit I'm her muse."

My accurate observation didn't sit too well with Java, who plucked a black olive from the nearest hors d'oeuvre tray and chunked it at my head. "I got your muse, jerk."

"No," I corrected, "Laken does."

"Hey, aren't we here to celebrate you becoming Mrs. Cross?" Derek squeezed Java's cheeks between his hands in a feeble play for peace that worked. Java gushed, melted and sank deep into his chest. I recognized that content look. It was the same way Laken used to look at me…just before breaking me off with some affection. A bit of jealousy pinched the back of my neck as they started smooching, but I shook it off.

"You know you're wrong, Knight." Java broke their sloppy lip-lock, rigid demeanor slowing her deep southern drawl more than usual.

"Wrong for what, Java? Protecting my art from that thief you call a friend?" I snapped.

"Hold up, bro – that thief is my sister." Derek sat straight in defense mode, scooting his bride-to-be to the edge of his lap. More 90's hip-hop blared through the speakers, but I was too unfocused to make out the playlist.

"No offense, Derek." I took off my shades and laid them on the table. "What your sister did was foul, though."

"Foul? No, what was foul was you screwing Laken's brains out until the contents of that creative little head of hers spilled out with your toy soldiers. She was vulnerable."

"Vulnerable, J?"

"Yes, vulnerable." Java jumped from Derek's lap; hands jammed on her hips. "She was helpless. You hit a women's happy place and she's liable to tell you anything."

"Anything except how to keep her supposed best friend from telling all of her business."

I didn't know when Laken crept up on us, but the bass in her normally airy voice put fear in me that I hadn't experienced since I was a kid, sitting with the Mother's Board in church on Sunday mornings. Those old ladies were mean, but they didn't have anything on Laken. Memories of her scaling the walls of her childhood home, ambushing me and Derek made me shiver. Laken could fight and I hadn't worked out in a while. I needed a good head start just to outrun her.

"Could you be less forthcoming with what we've discussed in the dark, Java?" Laken playfully punched her friend in the arm, but we all knew she wasn't kidding.

"Well, what's done in the dark…" Java countered.

"…is cliché, just like Laken's writing," I said. I would've given half my royalties just to freeze Laken's bewildered expression in time.

Priceless.

"Not to mention, baby sis is miffed that she's still punching the clock at Frisco Farms while I got CEO of Knight in Armor Publishing embroidered on my chest. Full time. Laken's not jealous of me...but she's got mad envy for my pen."

"You son-of-a-" Laken lunged toward me and I wasted no time scooting from within her reach.

"Guys, you're blowing my buzz." Derek hopped to his feet, thankfully blocking his sister from swatting me. Laken was tiny, but effective. "Listen, I love you both but I love my future wife even more. We're about to hit the buffet, school these younguns on the dance floor, and take our behinds home. I suggest you do the same."

"Wait, you're leaving us?" my normally masculine voice sputtered like first name Wimpy, last name Kid.

"Grown man status," Derek reprimanded. He jokingly put a fist to both of his eyes, silently instructing Laken how to handle me. "I'm done jumping in business that doesn't pay me."

Before either if us could protest, Derek smacked Java's behind and sauntered off, grooving toward the dance floor. My food deprived stomach called after them, but I doubted they could hear it rumbling over the bass in the music. Laken's demented grimace sent my sweat glands out of control. My costume was drenched. I slid off my plaid blazer, eyes alert for any sudden movement coming from the other side of the table. When it came to women, I was rarely caught unprepared.

...except when that woman was Laken.

Laken rapped her French tips on the table, off-beat drumming clashing with the music. Those nails used to feel good running across my back; now they sounded like retribution. Between her eerie squint, hollow grin, and stiff posture, I silently prayed my name was included in the

Lamb's Book of Life, unsure if I'd make it out the club on two feet and not a stretcher. One of my legs bobbed up and down so fast, it felt like I was running sideways in my seat. I knew Laken's temper was as short as she was, but dang. This wasn't the type of adrenaline we'd enjoyed in the past; nice-nasty wasn't appealing fully clothed.

Laken pulled a tablet from her oversized bag and powered it on. She scrolled in silence, staring a moment before pushing out a heavy sigh. She glanced from the tablet to me, dropped her head and began reading.

"After our first encounter in the back of her Uber, Tristan consistently hit me up every Tuesday." Laken recited in monotone. "A Monday text from "T" meant full bellies and legs up come Tuesday. *Taco Tuesday* was new to me. Up until this point, I thought it was choosing between hard or soft shells, spicy or mild, street or Tex-Mex. Nothing more than munchies and memes. Tristan's culinary celebrations triggered fantasies my prepubescent mind had only imagined. We flipped Tuesdays into steamy torture that I never wanted to stop. This enticing goddess did things to my body only meant to repeat during confession.

The last Tuesday we shared – the day before she abandoned me, Tristan didn't bring any food. The erotic devices and diversions were absent when she appeared on my doorstep. Her leather backpack wasn't even hanging off her rain-soaked shoulders. Hair drenched, thin, polka dot dress stuck to her skin; every curve sang its own song. The disconnect of her sullen demeanor failed to resonate with me. Everything about her was familiar, until it wasn't. That night, there was no pomp and circumstance to our lovemaking. Just Tristan in my favorite white t-shirt and nothing else sprawled on my king-sized bed, Boomerang playing on the television, and all the indiscretions I wouldn't regret in the morning. The only thing I regretted was letting her get away."

Laken slowed down when she came to parts of the story which I obviously borrowed from the truth. That humble pie was so dry it wouldn't budge, not even with the ice water I guzzled to help wash it down. Laken shanked me with my own prose. The tablet dropped with a thud when she tossed it back into her bag. I wasn't sure whether to speak or run.

"You want everyone to think I'm jealous of your success, Knight." Laken emphasized success with air quotes. "Problem is, you and I both know your bestselling fiction is my miserable truth."

My leg started jumping again. I wished it was for a different reason. "Miserable? You? You never came back, Laken. You never came back"

There it was. My part of our reality.

Laken stiffened and rocked in her seat, pushing an empty glass back and forth across the table. She studied me, trying to discern the truth from a lie. Her full lips pursed and caramel cheeks turned bright crimson before countering, "I couldn't."

I pressed a hand down on my leg to force the vibrating to stop. I gulped more water, even though I needed something a lot stronger to make me forget the calls sent straight to voice mail, the unanswered text messages, and DMs that sat unread. I drank more, pretending not to be bothered by the way had Laken ghosted me. Especially since I never got to tell her how much I loved her crazy tail.

Laken

Knight knew I was coming to the party as Whitley. That's the only reason that sucka pulled a Dwayne Wayne on me.

Sitting across from me, looking like more:

More of his kisses.

More of his body.

More of his touch.

More of his…

Focus, girl. Stay focused, I scolded myself.

"Creep" by TLC provided the soundtrack for our confrontation, the furthest thing from coming to Jesus. There was nothing celestial about the venomous way my literary rival and I glared at each other. This meeting of offenses hurt like hell.

Despite the fact that he was scared senseless, Knight slowly swayed to the music. Probably to distract me. I'd forgotten what a wonderful dancer he was. Didn't matter. The last thing I wanted to do was dance, trade spit or anything else that required a human touch with Knight Brad- *my Lamb, his smile was more delectable than ever.*

"Hey," he snapped his fingers in my face. "Laken? Laken?"

"Sorry," I mumbled. "You were saying?"

"I was reminding you how you ripped me up like a losing scratch-off ticket."

In spite of myself, I laughed. First time I found humor in Knight's presence in a long while. His heavy chuckle conjoined with mine; the only two things about us to touch and agree, since –

"How long are you going to make me wait, Lake?" Knight swirled a Tootsie Roll between his fingers, head tilted. I shook off the memory of him kneading my thighs the way he worked that candy.

"Wait for what?" I asked.

"How long are you going to wait to tell me why you disappeared?"

"I'll think about it…when you explain why on earth you would write the last night we spent together in that book of yours."

I was grateful the DJ came over the loud speaker, announcing a break in the music, so I could hear Knight's bull response clearly. His chiseled face contorted; he stroked his beard, conjuring up his tall tale.

"Why wouldn't I write about the woman who turned me out?" Knight's dark lips curled into a smile I could barely resist. But he wasn't getting off that easy.

"Turned you out? Please." I rolled up the sleeves of my blazer. "Man, if my brother knew what really went down – or came up, between us…you'd still be in intensive care, eating dinner from an IV."

I looked past Knight in time to see my girl Java showing off her ring to a group of ladies hanging at the cash bar. I loved how she loved Derek; pure, intense. They deserved each other. She was an incredible woman and my brother was a stand-up dude. What they had was what I wanted for myself. But after I walked away from Knight, it seemed like no other man could compare.

Knight ruined me for all brothers.

In more ways than one.

I cleared my throat, and let the response escape as concisely as I could. "I can attribute some of the most inti- mate moments of my life to you, Knight. You were the first boy I beat up."

"Hey, I let you," Knight argued playfully.

"Yeah, we'll let that be your testimony," I said. "Any- way, you were also my first kiss at Homecoming and the first man I made love to. You were also the first to know about my wanting to be an author. Because I told you after the third time we made love."

"You were counting?" Knight's brows rose in curiosity.

"Knight," I snapped.

"Just clarifying."

"Anyway - after a while, things didn't feel right." My confession rolled off my tongue more gruffly than I intended. "*Two Became One*."

Knight had the nerve to twist his face into a quizzical scowl rather than ask me to remind him what he'd obviously forgotten. I sucked my teeth, took a napkin from the table and shredded it in my hands.

"*Two Became One* was the short story I submitted for the campus literary journal. The same story about strangers hooking up under extreme circumstances, which served as the foundation of *Uber Intentions*." I paused, because the more I recalled, the more I wanted to plant my fist right in the crease of Knight's dimpled chin. "The same story I read to you naked over street tacos with habanero salsa. Just before you had the epiphany to ditch your aspirations of becoming a veterinarian for a career as an author."

"Are you serious?" The bass in Knight's voice delved deep, like his hands used to do to me on Tuesdays. "You knew I loved writing, Laken. Books are what brought us together in the first place."

"Books brought us together, not whoring the craft of writing for a few royalties."

"Consistent royalties," Knight corrected with a wink.

I slammed my fist on the table to resist from connecting it to my former lover's smug face. "This isn't a joke, Knight. You know I've always been serious about this. For you, writing was a grade and a hobby. Words on the page were meant to be a way out for me." I tried not to sound whiny, but my emotions betrayed me, just like Knight. A few tears spilled from my eyes, dripping onto my baby pink blazer.

Dang.

Knight reached across the table, handing me a handkerchief to dry off. Reluctantly, I conceded. His hand grazed mine when I accepted his peace offering, sending a familiar surge that I'd missed dearly. I snatched my hand away, dabbing my eyes with the plaid cloth.

"Listen, I didn't know it was that deep for you," Knight said.

"It doesn't matter much now, does it?" My lungs felt like they were being squished. I tried to breathe without dropping more tears before snapping, "You're the big-time author now. All I am is a receptionist who slings clichés for kicks."

"Hey, who said you're a bad writer?" Knight asked.

"You did. Remember?"

Knight bit his bottom lip and slunk in his seat. It was obvious he wanted to take his words back, but just like our entire relationship – or lack thereof, the universe grabbed hold of our recklessness. We sat in silence, me sniffling and Knight sighing over and over. He finally leaned forward and gently took my hand – the one without the soiled cloth, in his. His pillow soft lips grazed my skin. Three times. Because he did most things in threes.

"I'm sorry, Laken. I didn't mean to degrade your gift. You know I realize your pen is blessed. Maybe I'm the one who's envious."

I hadn't seen this level of sincerity in Knight since our last Taco Tuesday. The one where I deliberately acted out my plan to break his heart. Mission accomplished.

…except I got wounded in the process.

"Thank you," was all I could manage to say.

"I mean it, Laken. You're a talented writer. Well, storyteller. But you refused to write the last chapter with me. I guess I just wanted to borrow some of the magic that made me fall in love with you."

My eyes bugged. Did I hear right? Maybe the music was too loud. That was it. Doggone Johnny Gill was keeping me from hearing straight. I needed Mr. Bradley to repeat himself.

"Say what?" I stated more than asked.

"We were young enough to play games when we were hooking up at CU, Laken." Knight explained. "Now we're too old and life is short. I've never met another woman I wanted as much as I want you."

"Wedding fever," I awkwardly laughed off his admission. "Commitment becomes a thing when someone besides you is taking the leap."

"This isn't about Derek and Java. I'm talking about picking up where we left off." Knight leaned close enough for his fresh breath to tickle my nostrils. "I'm not proposing anything, Laken. I'm just saying – at least consider writing the end of the story we started. Together."

Doubt pressed against my ribcage. "If you thought we had something – something worth exploring, then why did you let me go, Knight?"

"Because sometimes it's best that when someone wants to go, you let them. I won't make that mistake again."

Without another word, Knight twined his fingers in my waves with a slight tug. He cradled my head with one hand; used the other to slowly run a finger from my forehead, gliding past my eyes and down the bridge of my nose, parking on my lips. My heart accelerated, thumping hard beneath the soft strokes. All at once, I was transported back to my dorm room, curled between Knight's legs, allowing him to entice me with books and breakfast. Geesh, I just knew this man was everything I wanted. But I demoted myself to a consistent booty call before he had the chance to. I missed those days. Too bad I chose to hate Knight for following his end of the dream instead of making room for his success so we could love.

Knight discreetly kneaded my scalp, stared intensely and pressed those wonderful lips into mine. I accepted his apology, his tongue, his heat. My mind swirled, body went limp, giving in even more. Knight dove deeper into my mouth, giving me what he knew I wanted in front of my brother, bestie, and the angels who were surely giving me the side-eye.

…and I never flinched.

CHAPTER THREE

When it's Broken...Love it

Knight

"Bevvy lay on her side, back to me. A slight snore escaped her lips. She wouldn't be lucid any time soon. I couldn't resist running my hand down her naked spine as it contracted with her even breaths. She was so warm, so peaceful. I loved how her skin felt on my hands. How she awakened parts of me that grief tried its hardest to bury. How she poured herself into her art, but made room to connect with my heart. How she accepted my flaws and adjusted my crown without the rest of the world knowing. Bevvy was sensible, romantic, and free. It was hard to be negative in her presence; her eclectic vibe diminished the myth of the angry black woman generations before her carved out. I couldn't stand to be out of her presence…but I worked hard every day to be present. I brushed her golden cornrows from her shoulder, planting kisses in all the places I'd claimed an hour earlier. She stirred a bit when I pulled her into me; moaned and reached for my hand. Pulled it to her lips, reciprocating her feelings through her love language. This was the woman I'd prayed for. The woman who restored me."

Laken closed the paperback with a heavy sigh after reading the last sentence. She ran her hands across the glossy cover, admiring the sensual photo of the intertwined couple on the front: the woman's nude, arched back in full view, her lover's arms around her waist. The photo told a story of its own – black love did exist. Laken's fingers skated back and forth over the picture, stopping only to trace the title: *RECLASSIFIED - A Contemporary Romance. Knight Bradley & Laken Cross-Bradley.*

Laken removed her glasses and set them on the nightstand. "Babe – is there any part of our romantic life that isn't sacred?"

I knew what she was referring to, but with my wife, it was always best to play it safe. "I don't know what you're talking about?"

Laken rewarded my blissful ignorance with a slug to the shoulder. "I want to know why all of your chapters in the book we wrote together recount our sexual history in thinly veiled detail?"

"Whoa, woman – there's more than a few of your chapters that play back our memories like a VHS tape," I defended. "And they weren't exaggerated if I say so myself." I massaged the part of me that pleased her most for emphasis.

"Cretin." Laken took one of the pillows propped behind her head and smacked me with it.

"Hey, chill out. We don't want Baby Bradley to pick up his mommy's violent tendencies."

"Hopefully, *she* won't inherit her father's gargantuan head."

Laken rested her hands on her protruding belly. Her maternal glow illuminated the darkness from the heavy drapes blanketing the hotel room that was our home for the next few days. The Sip-N-Read Book Club spared no expense bringing us from Dallas to St. Louis for their annual Lit Affair Weekend – one of the largest romance novel jams in the country. I'd been in the past as a solo author, but this was Laken's first time.

As a best-selling author.

With me.

I shook my head, astounded how a little faith trans-formed my former sometimes lover from wanting to kill me into a wife and writing partner. Laken was right - Derek and Java's engagement party was a catalyst for reconnec-tion. After that kiss, the one that brought us back together, we went back to my place. In an Uber. There was a bit of fussing (Laken), followed by cursing (again, Laken) but our words turned into action, and those actions were…well, they were between us. Me and my wife.

…because we wasted no time getting down to the cour-thouse so I could give Laken my last name.

Right before we made a baby.

And wrote a romance.

Which readers devoured.

And retired Laken the receptionist upon becoming an overnight literary sensation.

No longer competing scribes, we co-authored life, together.

I ran my hands over my growing fro, which needed more than a little attention. We flew in on Thursday. Between speaking on various panels, signing books, and running around town to grab goodies to curb Laken's flamboyant cravings, I barely had time to bathe, much less properly groom. By Saturday, I was exhausted. This was our last day in the city, but my "honey do" list was longer than the conference itinerary. Watching my boo so healthy, happy, and content made the hassle worth it, though. Laken was an incredible wife. I knew she was going to be an amazing mother.

I yawned and got off the bed, looking at the clock on the wall to check the time. 10:12. That didn't leave much time to grab my wife's food before the first session, but I was determined to figure it out. I pulled a white t-shirt over my head and slid into the jeans I planned on wearing to the event.

"I'm famished. Hurry up and get dressed so we can get my duck fried rice and White Castle before the signing."

"Don't rush me," I playfully scolded. "You're the one who stopped me from getting ready so we could have story time. And they're going to have lunch there, babe."

Laken's brows shot up as she pointed a finger at me. "Are you going to deprive the woman who's been pregnant with your baby for the last thirteen months? I don't care what the sisters have," Laken cradled her belly, "we want what we want." She hunched forward like she was in pain, but I was used to that from her. We'd both grown in the two years of wedded bliss, but one thing hadn't changed: my wife was extra and dramatic.

"Ma'am — you have not been pregnant thirteen months," I laughed. "I realize you're ready to drop this baby, but let's just get through the weekend, get back home, and get you on bed rest until she comes."

Laken slid off the bed onto her feet. She scrunched her face and shoved both hands on her back. "She...you said she. See, I told you we're having a girl."

"No I didn't," I fussed. "I clearly said he. And you will not make my son feel bad for your lack of discernment, woman." I was joking, but Laken's face was serious. It was that the same expression the nine-year-old with frizzy pigtails and buck teeth had before she jumped on my back and took me out. Only now, Laken was a stunning woman, who loved me and our –

"Knight," Laken grumbled through clenched teeth. She waddled to the desk across from her, grabbed the edge and hunched forward. I was next to her in two steps.

"Babe, you alright?"

"Do I look alright?" Laken rolled her eyes. She breathed hard, like she couldn't get enough air. "It's hot in here, huh?"

"You want some water?"

"No...I want my Castles. And my rice." Before Laken could finish barking her order for the tenth time that morning, sweat poured from every part of her body like she was standing under a sprinkler. She grabbed her stomach with a howl that I was certain shook the entire third floor of the hotel. I tried to help her, but Laken pushed me away. She couldn't stand up straight, bent over yelling obscenities and hurling insults that I hoped were just being said in the heat of the moment.

I wasn't sensitive...but some of those shots fired hurt, man.

"Knight. It's. Time." Laken's speech was stilted. She yanked me down to her level by the tail of my shirt and looked me in the eyes. "We gotta go, honey."

Panic raged through every part of me that was awake.

Muscles I hadn't exercised in years were suddenly sore and trying to get my attention. I began sweating harder than she was. "Wait – we're not ready. I mean, we're in St. Louis, everything we have for the baby is at home…the conference."

"The sisters will understand, Knight," Laken groaned, then managed to smile through the pain, which seemed to be more frequent. "We're about to have our book baby."

"Our baby," I repeated. "Our baby is coming. And we're not even at home." I started to panic.

Laken panted, took my hand in hers and squeezed. Again – the little woman was stronger than she looked. "It doesn't matter where we are, honey. I'm just happy to be having this baby with you."

I helped my wife to the bed; grateful she was already dressed. Getting her out of her clothes had never been an issue; I was in no state of mind to get her clothes back on. I slipped her sandals on her feet, pulled her braids into a ponytail at the nape of her neck and threw my tennis shoes on. When I realized the shoes were on the wrong feet, I snatched them off and replaced them correctly. All the while, Laken's groans grew louder and louder. I knew it was too close for Baby Bradley to make his or her appearance in the world to travel like this, but Laken had insisted. *"I've waited too long to be a full-time author,"* she'd told me, *"Me and this baby are going to enjoy every minute."*

I fumbled around the room, until Laken snapped, "Calm down, Knight."

I froze, took a deep breath, and waited to feel the blood circulating in my body. I walked to the bed, squatted in front of Laken and gently kissed her forehead. It was sweeter than our first kiss. "What do you need me to do?" I asked.

Laken looked at me, smiled and said, "Get an Uber."

THE END

ABOUT CANDICE JOHNSON

Candice "Ordered Steps" Johnson spins stories of love, loss and overwhelming faith. Her creativity isn't simply hidden between the pages; she's an Emmy-winning choreographer, dancer and filmmaker who uses art to survive. Practice What You Praise (which is also a short film), Only Tithes Will Tell and Catching Feelings for Christmas are but a few of her titles. She wears her heart on her pen and hangs hope in creating.

Connecting is her passion & she'd love to hear from you: candiceosp@gmail.com, bit.ly/candiceosp

 facebook.com/candiceyjohnsonauthor

 twitter.com/AuthorCandiceJ

 instagram.com/naturaldancer

RESTORED

SABRINA B. SCALES

Ten years after their bad break-up, Deja and Orlando are forced to spend time together. As expected, tensions are high and it's impossible to imagine reconciliation after such a long rift. Will Lando and Deja be able to restore what was lost or will they continue down two paths leading in opposite directions?

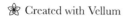

CHAPTER ONE

Deja

My mother didn't name me Deja Blu until the moment I was born. She said that nothing had come to mind until she looked into my eyes, two earthy pools of wonder staring at her like they knew who she was. I used to sit in her salon, spinning around in the vacant chair next to her station that had once belonged to her mother, but was now and forever empty because even in death, my grandmother was intimidating. I'd listen to Mama telling all of her clients about my pretty brown face being a symbol of God's grace and how He always restored what was lost. I didn't know then but I found out later, that wasn't something she'd read from a book of affirmations. Mama'd suffered deeply before I came into this world, losing a baby boy to a miscarriage three years before my birthday, and a baby girl one year later to the same untimely circumstances.

Sitting on the bottom step of the house I'd grown up in, I was reminded of life's fragility and how quickly things could change. A neighbor had stopped by to see why Mama hadn't collected her newspaper from the driveway, then pushed the front door open to find her lying nearly lifeless on her bedroom floor. No foul play was involved, thankfully. Just a stubborn woman who'd refused to take her meds, seeking attention from a workaholic husband who'd be back to his old ways as soon as she recovered. I'd like to say that this scenario surprised me, but the truth was it hadn't at all. Dysfunction was the name of the game under our roof.

Some considered it saddening.

We considered it Sunday.

"You alright out here, baby girl?" Daddy'd finished up dinner for the two of us and from the smell coming out of the door, he'd cleaned the kitchen too.

"Yes, sir." I looked up and over my shoulder at the tall, brown skinned man with the salt and pepper beard, who'd been my personal superhero for thirty two years, no matter how far away his powers had to travel.

"You don't look like it." He made his way down the recently replaced steps, taking a seat beside me and resting his forearms on his knees. "It's not your fault. You know that right?"

"Of course, I know that, Daddy. But it doesn't change the fact that she's in the hospital with tubes running from everywhere." I took in a deep breath and leaned forward to rest my elbows on my thighs and my face in the palms of my hands.

"Why can't you just work from home?" I turned my head to the side and asked him. "You've been running Huffington's for thirty years and you can't take a break to be at home with your wife?"

"It's not that easy, Baby Girl." He gave his typical excuse. "If I'm not where I need to be, things could crumble. Everything we've worked for, everything we've built to leave behind for you and DJ, would fall into the pits. Is that what you want?"

"What I *want* is for my mother to live and not die from a broken heart while you're out workin' or whatever you wanna call it." I sat up straight then stood to head up the steps.

"Excuse me, what did you just say?" Daddy hopped up off the steps way too fast for a sixty-year-old man.

"Seriously, Daddy?" I kept on going, walking through the door that he'd left wide open. "I'm not a little girl anymore. I know you're not spending days at a time away from home for *work*."

"Deja, you better be careful what you're saying right now." His voice stiffened as he entered the kitchen behind me.

"I know *exactly* what I'm saying. And so do you." I turned around to face him, tears weighing heavy and ready to fall from my eyes.

"I know you love her." I said as he stood there shocked and silent. "Even though she makes it hard sometimes. Why do you think I never come home? I don't wanna deal with it either."

"Baby Girl—"

"I'm not mad at you, Daddy." I cut him off. "You do what you have to do and that's none of my business. But she needs you now. She needs *us* now. And I can't do this by myself. I already have enough on my plate."

"Ok." He nodded, grabbing me by the hand and pulling me against his side. "And I'm sorry." He squeezed me tight, causing a fountain of tears to pour down my cheeks, soaking into his t-shirt.

"One question." I sniffed, running a finger across my runny nose as the tears subsided.

"Go ahead." He pushed away and looked down into my eyes.

"Is it Miss Harris?" I looked up at my daddy, already wearing a smirk.

"What? No! Heavens no! Why would you... never mind that. No, it's not Miss Harris." He planted a kiss on my forehead and headed to the stove to fix our plates.

"Thank God." I breathed out a sigh of relief. "She'd be a terrible bonus mother."

*

It was ten o'clock at night and I'd been staring at the door for an hour, waiting for his car to pull up in the driveway. I hated tardiness as much as I hated wet bread in my dishwater, but he'd never respected that, which was one of the reasons we weren't together in the first place. Just when I'd decided to pick up the phone and call, a set of headlights shone through the window beside the front door and music played loud enough to wake every neighbor down the block.

Stupid asshole.

"Is that that boy?" Daddy came down the hallway looking as annoyed as I felt.

"You know it." I stood from the sofa and headed toward the door.

"I can't tell you how glad I was when you finally came to your senses." He chuckled. "Boy ain't got the good sense God gave a horsefly." He shook his head and took a seat in his Lazy Boy, flipping on the TV.

I laughed and hurried to the door, the sound of two sets of boots hurrying up the steps pulling my heart in two different directions. I pulled the door open after hearing a tiny signature knock toward the bottom, my smile spreading a mile wide at the sight of my little boy.

"DJ!" I cheered like I always did. There was no way I could look down into those big brown eyes without lighting up with joy no matter how bad my day had been.

"Mommy!" He opened a pair of long arms that he'd inherited from his lanky father, allowing me to sweep him up off the ground and hug him so, so tight.

"I missed you so much," I whispered in his ear. "Did you miss me?" I tilted my head back to ask.

"Yes ma'am." He grinned, displaying the huge space where his two front teeth used to be. "Daddy took me to see Grammie Gene and she misses you, too," he said so casually, as if it hadn't been a whole year since the last time I'd seen my ex's mother.

"Desmond." I acknowledged the light eyed man who had once occupied every crevice of my thoughts.

"Wassup, D?" He tipped his bony chin. "Like the hair." He extended a hand toward my face and an alarm must've gone off in my father's ear, pulling him from his seat in the other room and pushing him to where we were standing.

"Might be a good idea to keep our hands to ourselves, Mr. Howard." Daddy cleared his throat. And DJ's head popped up like popcorn at the sound of his grandpa's voice.

"Paw Paw, I didn't know you were here!" he cheered, sliding out of my arms and hurrying back to his grandfather.

"Whoa, whoa. You almost pushed me down!" Daddy joked. "You hiding some muscles under that coat? Lemme see." He leaned over and picked DJ up, cutting his eyes at Desmond as I stepped out of the way.

"Ma said she'd be happy to keep him while you get

settled," Desmond said, eyes glossed like he'd been smoking, when I knew damn well he hadn't been smoking with my baby in the car.

"That won't be necessary," Daddy butted in. "He'll be fine right here."

"Daddy, I—"

He talked over me. "I'm taking some time off. Didn't we just discuss that?"

"Yes. But—"

"Then it's settled." The man wasn't letting me get a word in edgewise. "If Desmond or anybody else wants to see DJ, they can call you and stop by." He planted a kiss on DJ's cheek and fixed his eyes on the man he probably hated more than the devil himself.

"Cool." Desmond nodded, knowing that when it came to my father, going back and forth wasn't an option. "I'll see ya later, D-Man." He reached his long arm past me and ruffled his fingers through DJ's curly afro.

"Ok, Daddy. I love you," DJ chirped, leaning sideways and inviting his father into a hug that his grandfather was having a hard time tolerating.

"I love you, too." Desmond kissed his son on the cheek, nodding his head at me and Daddy before turning to walk out of the door. And for reasons that had been eating at me since the day me and Desmond split, I wished I would've handled that situation better. He was terrible as a husband, but he was a good father to our son.

"Come on, D. Let's go get you a bath." I took my seven year old from my father's arms and put him down on the floor, peeling off the brand new coat his daddy'd bought him and hanging it on a coat tree beside the front door.

"But I'm sleepy, Mommy. Can I take a bath in the morning?" He whined the way he always did before bath time. I didn't know what the deal was with boys and filth, but it was popular amongst DJ's friends.

"Grammie Byrd and Paw Paw made sure you have clean sheets on your bed and you wanna climb on em with a stinky booty? I don't think so, Mister." I reached out for his hand, poking him in the side when he raised his hand to grab mine.

"Now tell Paw Paw good night, 'cause you're going straight to bed after we scrub you clean." I patted his butt as he hurried over to hug Daddy, then ran off down the hallway to gather his pajamas and bath toys.

"And Daddy," I said before heading off behind DJ, "thanks. But I don't need you to do that."

"Baby I'm just—"

"I know," I said, squeezing his hand, "but I don't need you to. Not anymore, okay?"

"Okay," he sighed. And I knew he didn't mean it, but it sounded good anyway, so I left it at that.

CHAPTER TWO

Orlando

"That face was made for TV. I don't know why you didn't take that job with Sports Central."

I'd been off the field investing in real estate and several other business ventures for all of two years and my mother still hadn't accepted the fact that her larger than life son was content working behind the scenes. She wasn't complaining about the money it brought in, though. Hadn't paid a mortgage since I hit the field with the San Antonio Runners and even after my career ending injury, she was still sitting pretty. I'd even taken over her coffee shop, *Aroma*, giving it a facelift and hiring a marketing strategist to bring her up to speed with today's competition. This lady was nothing if not a diva, and for some reason, she assumed I'd wanted to be one too.

"This *face* is gonna be deflated if you don't hurry up with those eggs," I complained. Fully grown, two months into thirty two, and I still swung by my mama's to eat breakfast every morning.

"Well, we wouldn't want *that*." She cut her eyes at me, scraping a good helping of scrambled eggs straight from the skillet onto my plate. "How's work or whatever you call it?" She left the table to grab the dish of bacon and bowl of grits that she'd left on the stovetop.

"I call it work and it's been pretty good, actually." I bit into a slice of crispy bacon as soon as she placed it on my plate.

"How would you know if you're never there?"

"If you're referring to *Aroma*, I'm there once a month," I chuckled, "I'm not good with the hover method. That's more your speed."

"Watch your mouth."

"I'm just sayin'."

"And so am I." She bucked a set of pecan brown eyes.

"And that's a shame." She took a seat beside me at the small table for four, pouring each of us a glass of fresh-squeezed orange juice. "Everybody's so used to being separate. This new school way of doing things is gonna leave us in a world of antisocial lunatics who don't know how to carry on a face to face conversation."

"It's not that bad, Ma." I smiled, swallowing down half a glass of juice. "Besides, *Aroma's* not the only place I have to look after. And look at us. Are we *not* having a face to face conversation?"

"We're only doing this because I've threatened you." She bucked her eyes again and I chuckled. "Won't be so easy for your little sister," she added on a nod.

And I couldn't believe she'd mentioned the one topic we'd been avoiding for the better part of seven years.

"And don't act all surprised. Nathaniel told me you've

been spending time with her," she added in response to the shocked look on my face.

"I've been spending time with Markie since she was born. That's never gonna change," I returned, "And since when did you and Pops start talking?"

"About a month ago," she sighed, "He stopped by for some papers he needed and I just happened to be in the garden. He's lucky I didn't have a hoe in my hands."

"Ma!"

"Don't *Ma* me. Your father's a trifling piece of shit. And I don't care how cute that little girl is, I will never welcome her into my house." Her voice had gone up and she'd pushed her plate away.

"And I'm not saying you should." I took a deep breath and laid my hand on top of hers. "Especially not while you have access to sharp objects," I teased and she pinched me. "All I'm saying is that it's not her fault the way she got here."

"And it's not mine either." She pulled her hand away. "Listen, I don't wanna talk about this. I fixed you a salad for lunch. It's in the refrigerator. I'm gonna go get ready for my yoga session." She stood from the table, still as slender as she'd been my whole life; butter-toned skin peppered with red freckles, gray streaks highlighting her shoulder length, dark brown waves. Gathering the plate of food that she'd barely touched, she headed into the kitchen to dump it down the garbage disposal

"Ma!" I yelled from the kitchen after scarfing down as much of the breakfast as I could before dumping the scraps and rinsing my plate.

"Yes." She stopped in the middle of the hallway and looked back at me.

"Thanks for breakfast," I said, walking up to her and

leaning in to kiss her forehead. "And lunch. I'll be by to check on you later, okay?"

"I'll hold you to it." She squeezed my hand. "And I love you, too."

Deja

Fall was my favorite season. Mostly because my birthday was in October, but also because the weather was perfect. Well, sometimes. In Houston, you wouldn't know what to wear until you walked outside and felt what season the Lord decided to drop down. On this morning I was lucky. Sixty-five breezy degrees finally gave me the chance to pull out a pair of slate-gray leather booties that I had stuffed into my luggage before the trip back home, to pair with a rose-gold blazer and gray fitted slacks, the ensemble for my first day at work.

"You don't have to bring him home. I'll swing by and pick him up after work." I bit into a bagel that I'd just spread cream cheese over, rushing to the door and looking down at my phone screen to realize that I'd been on the phone with Desmond for ten whole minutes.

If I didn't know any better, I'd swear the brother just wanted to hear my voice.

"Desmond, you hear me?" I asked when he didn't respond, grabbing my briefcase off the sofa and my keys out of the key box before heading out the door.

"Huh? Yeah. You'll get him after work. Cool."

"Cool. Will he be at your mom's or your place?" I asked. Desmond's living situation was still a little sketchy.

For the month that I'd been back in town, DJ was almost always at his mother's house.

"Ma's. He'll be at my mom's," he said, "You sure you don't need me to bring him?"

"Yes, I'm sure," I repeated for the third time, "Are you okay? You sound…different."

"Nah, I'm good," he huffed, "I just might not be over there when you pick him up and I wanted to see you. See *him* off."

"Oh." I caught that slip up that didn't really feel like a slip up. "I can have him FaceTime you before bed if you want," I suggested.

"Yeah, that's cool." He cleared his throat. "Have a good day, Deja," he greeted way too softly for the man who'd broken my heart and other parts into a million and one pieces.

"Thanks. You do the same." I pulled the phone from my ear, staring at it to make sure I'd been on the phone with the right person.

Shaking my head, I ended the call and dropped my cell in my purse before locking the door and hurrying out to my car.

*

"Surprise!"

I almost fell out of my damn shoes, walking into the office that had been my first job as a teen to find half the staff standing in the lobby blowing noise makers, surrounded by balloons and streamers.

"Jesus. Y'all did not have to do this!" I painted on a smile. Honestly, the last thing I wanted was a celebration. I'd never wanted to work for my father again after leaving for college. Yet here I was, standing in his building.

"Girl, please. You know you love a party." My best and oldest friend, Abbie, was the first to break from the crowd. Holding a cupcake in one hand and a gift bag in the other, she pulled me into a warm hug and rocked me from side to side.

"You look amazing," she whispered in my ear as the others hurried in our direction.

"I feel drained already," I whispered back, forcing that smile back on my face as Abbie released me into the welcoming arms of a dozen other employees.

"Oh my God, Deja. It is so good to have you here!" the chattiest receptionist anybody ever knew, Kimberly, squeaked. She'd been working at Huffington's Imagination Station for the last five years and fit perfectly into the over the top atmosphere.

"Hey, Kimberly. Thanks." I was going for chipper, but it came out flat. "It's good to see you, too." I accepted her hug and kiss on the cheek, walking away with my lips balled up as she watched me with an exaggerated smile on her face.

Kimberly was borderline creepy.

Though it had been a minute since the last time I visited the office, I was used to everybody's eyes on me. Being the daughter of a man who literally created a market for imagining extraordinary events, they probably wondered what magical powers I had in store. Unfortunately, my powers were all fizzled out, replaced by motherhood and an untimely divorce. I didn't wanna be at Huffington's any more than I wanted a hole in my head, but I also didn't wanna keep withdrawing money from my savings to support me and DJ until it was time for us to go back to Dallas. Nor was I about to take my father up on the offer to let him handle things while I was back at home. James Huffington was a good man. Would give anybody the shirt off his back if they asked. But his giving always came at a cost. I'd learned that lesson from my mother.

"So, your dad put you back here away from the crowd." Abbie had fallen in step beside me after the greetings from the crowd subsided. She led me down a hallway toward the back of the office lined with closed off cubicles and typical office shrubbery. The tapping of keyboards fell under the sound of soft music playing over the PA system. Then we finally arrived at our destination, damn near a mile from the office's front door.

"Before you go in there..." Abbie stepped in front of me, placing herself between me and the tall, blonde wooden door flanked by windows with closed blinds. "There's something you need to know." She bit down on a long, clear fingernail, signaling a big problem that I definitely didn't have the energy to deal with.

"Abbie, if there are more balloons in this office, I'm gonna strangle somebody." I sighed, still holding the cupcake and gift bag as well as a briefcase in my hands.

"No. No, it's not balloons," she assured me, her super light skin flushed red. "It's...it's um... it's a person." She twisted her fingers together nervously.

"Wait, so, I'm sharing an office with somebody?" My eye twitched. As if coming back to work at this ridiculously friendly establishment wasn't painful enough, I had to share an office too?

Wow!

"No. It's a client," she carefully added, bracing her palms behind her against the door.

"Abbie, I love you. But please move. At this point, the client could be Santa Claus and I wouldn't care." I reached past her waist and pushed the long door handle downward.

"Well, he does have a beard," she whispered through

closed lips, sliding out of the way as I pushed the door open.

The next thing I remembered was the scent of *Coffee Bean Beard Balm* swimming up into my nose. As a suggestion from me, my father had been placing it in the Christmas boxes of every one of his male employees for the last five years whether they had beards or not. What he didn't know was that that particular fragrance reminded me of someone. Someone who didn't drink coffee but always smelled like he did because he worked at his family's coffee shop in college and brought the aroma with him when he visited my dorm.

I stepped over the threshold following my nose, completely taken aback by who was standing beside my desk. My eyes went wide, cupcake tumbled to the floor, and my briefcase suddenly felt like it was six foot three and carrying two hundred and forty five pounds of muscle. It was no coincidence that those measurements perfectly described the man standing in the fairly spacious room that I'd be calling my office indefinitely. I'd committed that physique to memory my sophomore, junior, and senior years in college. Never had I ever expected to see that wavy haired, caramel faced, Frenchman looking negro anywhere close to me again. But there he was, Orlando Christopher Terry, standing less than twenty feet away.

Orlando

She'd aged like fine wine and I wasn't surprised. She looked just like her mother who didn't look a day over twenty five the last time I'd seen her. That long, charcoal hair that used to drape over her shoulders was now styled in a sexy pixie cut that complimented the almond shape of her face. A peep of her collarbone was exposed under an ice-white blouse that she wore beneath her blazer. Pecan brown skin called at me; and I knew for a fact it was as smooth as satin.

Bedroom eyes the color of cinnamon and stone stared right through me as if they couldn't believe I was there. And my eyes were probably doing the exact same thing. I knew she was coming, but nothing could ever prepare my heart for seeing Deja Blu.

"Is my father in his office?" She rolled her eyes from me to Abbie without acknowledging my presence.

"Yeah. I think he's in a mee——"

"He'll have to reschedule," she cut Abbie off. I knew this wasn't gonna go well, but I'd at least expected her to speak.

"I'm so sorry." Abbie apologized, face turning red. "She'll come around; I promise. I'm gonna go get somebody to clean up this mess." She backed out of the office, leaving the door open behind her. And all I could do was take a deep breath and wait.

*

Moments later, I heard a commotion coming back down the hallway; two distinctive voices belonging to Deja and her father. I hadn't prepared anything to say. It had been so long since me and Deja had spoken that finding the right thing would've been impossible. And as she stormed back into the office with her father right behind her, I straightened in my seat and waited for him to do all the work.

"Orlando, Deja has something to say to you," Mr. Huffington said, clearing his throat when Deja didn't speak on his cue.

She cleared her throat as well and struggled to say a single word. "Hmm, *hi.*"

"Hey. It's good to—"

"I spoke. Now can you refer him to somebody else?" She darted her eyes back to her father before I could finish my sentence.

"That wasn't the deal," Mr. Huffington replied. "Besides, it's the holiday season and all other agents are already overbooked. You're it, Baby Girl. And I'm sure Mr. Terry's gonna bring in some hefty clientele. It'd be nice if you thanked him."

"You're pushing it, Dad." She rolled her eyes and gathered her things, marching over to a sleek, white desk at the back of the office and dropping everything on top of it. "And I doubt the rest of the staff would be okay with the nicknames." She eased into her seat, powering on her laptop without looking up at either of us.

"Orlando, I apologize for my daughter's behavior," Mr. Huffington breathed out. "She'll be fine in a few days. In the meantime, I have a meeting to return to. Let me know if you need anything."

"I'm right here and I can speak for myself." Deja relaxed in the high-backed white leather chair that Mr. Huffington probably had custom-made just for her. *"There has to be another option,"* she said under her breath. Mr. Huffington didn't respond this time, instead bowing his head and leaving the office without speaking another word.

"Dej—"

"Just because I have to be in here with you does not mean that we have to talk," she snapped without looking up from the briefcase that she was rifling through.

"I get that," I returned on a sigh, "but it'd be a lot less awkward."

"You know what would also be a lot less awkward?" This time she looked up, and I'd be damned if those eyes didn't pull heat to the center of my chest. "If my father would get over you as fast I did."

Damn, that hurt. I didn't know if it was written on my face, but that shit definitely hit me in the gut.

"As you wish," I sighed, pulling out my phone, "I just sent the details. Hit me up if you got questions."

I turned and walked away, knowing that if I was getting this kind of customer service from somebody else I'd be taking my money and business elsewhere. But my sister wanted the Huffington's Imagination Station treatment. So, I bit my tongue and prepared for what was next.

CHAPTER THREE

Deja

"So that's it? You're just gonna sit in complete silence and never talk to the man at all?"

I hadn't been able to put a finger on what my father and Abbie had in common that kept her working at Huffington for the last ten years. But now, as I sat across the table from her at one of the tables in our dining area, I remembered. They both loved Orlando almost as much as they loved the idea of me *being* with Orlando. And her pressing me about being a bitch for the past week was a recipe for an argument that I didn't have the energy to have.

My mother was due to be released from the hospital today and I'd be leaving work early to make sure things were squared away at the house. Daddy had hired a nurse to be with her around the clock. Though she completely mobile, he no longer trusted her to keep up with her meds and he'd gotten chewed out about it at the hospital loud enough for the entire third floor ICU to hear.

"That's the plan," I said through a mouth full of crispy buffalo wings from the onsite restaurant that was one of the things, if not the only, I'd actually missed about working at Huffington.

"That's mean." Abbie smirked. "Lando's one of the good ones and you're letting something from ten years ago stop you from seeing that."

"He cheated, Abbie. You act like it was involuntary." I ripped open a packet of lemon scented wipes and cleaned the spicy red sauce from my fingertips.

"First of all, you don't have proof of that," she argued, "And second, have you seen him? The man got even finer since college. That beard alone is grounds for forgiveness."

Whether I liked it or not, Abbie was right. Ten years hadn't tarnished Orlando's striking good looks. Dark eyes that drank up everything around them. Caramel skin accented by chocolate freckles that danced on his cheeks and wide nose. Full pink-tinted lips that had kissed me so deep that if I closed my eyes, I could feel them right now. It took some time apart and a few years in an abusive relationship to realize that aside from living under my father's roof, the safest place I'd ever been was wrapped up in Lando's arms.

Until I was replaced.

Some stick figure sorority bitch had him all wrapped up in a corner after a homecoming game during our senior year. I told myself not to be pressed about it because Orlando drew chicks like moths to a flame. It would've been easier to sever ties while we were still young, before things got too serious.

Problem was, they were already too serious. At least they were on my end. We'd spent holidays together, met each other's families and the whole nine. But when he'd declined to defend himself against my constant accusations, I'd just assumed he didn't care and broke things off.

"You agree, don't you!?" Abbie's laughter pulled me out of my head. "You've been sitting at that desk lusting for a whole week. I know it. I can see it in your eyes." She flipped a cherry tomato across the table, hitting the side of my arm.

"The only thing you're seeing in my eyes is exhaustion, heffa." I thumped the tomato back across the table. "And me and him are way past reconciliation anyway."

"Maybe for you." She hiked a brow.

"Excuse me?" I snapped.

"You're mean."

"I am not!"

"Yes, you are!" She raised her voice, sleek chocolate ponytail seemingly tightening on top of her head. "And it's childish, seriously." She took a sip from her green tea.

"So now I'm mean *and* childish? Thanks a lot, friend."

"You're very welcome." She smacked her lips. "And as a *friend*, I suggest you fix your attitude. Because whether you like him or not, Orlando Terry's a paying customer. Don't cheat yourself on coins letting your emotions get in the way."

"Whatever." We both pushed our chairs back and stood from the table, gathering our plates and glasses and turning them in at the dishwasher's window.

"Whatever's gonna have you broke." She slid her eyes to the side at me, licorice-colored heels clacking against the polished linoleum floors. "Or do you think Desmond's child support'll keep you afloat until you run back off into the D-Town sunset?" She flashed a cheeky smile.

"Anybody ever told you you're nosy as fuck?" I asked as we exited the dining area.

"On a daily basis." She pinched my waist. "Hey, where are you going?" she asked as I took a right toward my father's office instead of a left toward my own.

"To talk my dad into swapping my client," I informed her, "This little matchmaker shit has gone on long enough."

Orlando

"I'm guessing it didn't work?"

Deja stormed into the office twenty minutes after her lunch break, wind from the door she slammed behind her sending a stack of papers flying off the file cabinet beside her door.

"What the hell are you doing in my office?" She propped a hand on her hip.

"Standing appointment," I replied, "The receptionist said you were onsite for lunch, so she let me in. Is that a problem?"

"Yes," she spat, kneeling down on the floor to gather up her mess. "But you're here. And the rules haven't changed so, please, stop talking to me."

I stood from my seat in the waiting area of her office, heading in her direction. "Look, I tried to tell your pops this was a bad idea. But he's as stubborn as you." I stooped down beside her and grabbed what was left of the papers from the floor, so close that I could smell her soft perfume.

"Thanks, but I got this." She snatched the papers from my hands, standing straight up and leaving me in a squat by myself.

"How long do you plan on doing this?" I got up and straightened my slacks, shoving my hands into my pockets as I stood before her desk.

"As soon as my mom's well, I'm going back to Dallas. So approximately *that* long." She flipped her eyes up at me; full, brimmed lips in need of a sweep of Carmex.

Just as I'd decided to back away and return to my seat, she reached into her purse and pulled out a tube of lip balm. That tiny, predictable action brought a smile to my face. I shook my head and walked away, seeing her glaring at me from the corner of my eye.

"Somethin' funny?" she asked as I sat down.

"Nah." I wiped the smile off my face.

"Then why were you smiling?" she kept on. This was the most I'd heard her speak since she got here.

"What, I can't smile now either? Am I gonna need a checklist?"

"You know what, never mind." She raised a hand dismissively. "Childish," she mumbled under her breath. And I almost let that slide. But the grown man in me wouldn't allow it.

"What's childish is sitting in silence every time I come up here."

"If you don't like the silence, ask my boss to pair you with someone else," she returned.

"Or, you could stop being unprofessional and do your damn job."

"Did you know it was me?" She bent her neck slightly. "Did you hop on board with this idea out of spite, Orlando?"

The way she said my name made me pause to catch myself before I responded the way I used to and sucked the words off her tongue.

"I didn't know you were gonna be my planner until a

week before the consultation. And I don't have a reason to be spiteful toward you. Nor do you have a reason to be spiteful toward me, other than the fact that you apparently enjoy it."

She closed her laptop and looked straight across the room, staring into my eyes in a way that made me nervous. Had I finally unearthed something that would make this woman talk? Or was I about to get told off in three separate paragraphs?

"You think I'm being spiteful?" she asked sounding legitimately confused.

"Yeah." I hiked my brows. "I mean how else do you explain a decade of silence? You won't even accept my friend request on Facebook."

"First of all, do you know how many spam accounts are open in your name?" She curled her lips to the side, lip balm popping, making me smile again.

"You could easily verify my identity. But we both know that's not the issue." I straightened in my seat, hands folded on my lap, legs spread in either direction.

"Oh really?" she piped.

"Yes really," I returned.

"Then what's the issue? I mean since you know all of a sudden."

"There's nothing sudden about it. You're mad about some shit from college. And you've held on to it so long it's a part of who you are."

"What's the shit?" she asked, face tensing with anger. "The shit I'm so mad about. Tell me in your own words exactly what it is."

I huffed out a chuckle. "I'm not doing this."

"Oh, *now* you're not doing this?" She stood up and approached me from the other end of the room, thick curves on full display beneath a form-fitting yellow dress, folding her arms across her chest and tapping her fingers against her skin.

"You said you wanted to talk. So, let's talk," she continued, "Let's throw it all out on the table so it's not hanging over our heads like a fucking rain cloud."

"Fine." I looked up at her, enjoying the silhouette of the outfit for the day.

She was beautiful; exquisite in every way. And she knew that shit too. It's why she had me over here willing to do anything to get back in her good graces.

"You got it all twisted, Deja," I said, still sitting. Still staring into a set of eyes that had haunted my dreams for so long I almost couldn't believe they were real.

"So you're saying I'm crazy?" she fumed, "You're saying I didn't walk into a party and catch you huddled up in a corner with some random bitch that looked nothing like me? 'Cause there were witnesses, Lando. So if I'm crazy, if I was fucking hallucinating, so were they."

I stood from my seat. Noticing the heightened pitch and shakiness in her voice made me wanna get closer. To comfort her if she'd let me and make sure she was ok.

"It wasn't like that." I stepped up beside her. The nude heels she was wearing put her head level with my cheek. "I mean it was, but… it's hard to explain."

"You've had plenty of time to practice." She folded her arms tighter, resting her behind on a small desk to the right of the office door, looking up at me. "Shoot."

I traced my tongue across my lips and rested my behind against the desk beside her. "It *was* me," I said, "I mean, I know you knew that, but you don't know why."

"Then tell me." She looked up the slope of my shoulder straight into my eyes. "Tell me why you were there with somebody else when you knew I could walk in at any moment. I'm literally dying to hear it."

On a deep sigh, I decided to tell the truth. It was all I had going for me after all this time, and honestly, it was the only option. I fell in love with Deja the first time I sat behind her in Humanities. And that love hadn't gone away or faded on my part, not even with the distance between us.

"I was scared," I said in a voice that I didn't recognize as my own.

"Of what?" She stood up straight and dropped her arms to the side.

"It's gonna sound stupid." I shoved my hands into the pockets of my slacks and crossed my legs at the ankles, watching Deja's eyes following them before she tried to play it off.

She quickly brought her eyes up. "Because it probably is. But say it anyway."

"You knew my situation. At home, I mean."

"And you knew mine too. But that's no excuse."

I stared down at the floor. "I know. But it's the only explanation I have for being stupid. I didn't believe in healthy relationships, Deja. I didn't even know what that was. And I just…what we had scared me, I guess. Felt like I'd just fuck it up."

"So, you fucked it up out of fear of fucking it up? That makes zero sense. You know that right?"

"I do *now*." I shrugged. "But we were kids then. Logic wasn't my strongest attribute."

"You know what, it doesn't matter." She flipped both hands up and headed back to her desk. "Thanks for finally telling me the truth, though."

"You're welcome, I guess." I blew out a breath and leaned against the desk awaiting further instruction.

"You don't think I deserved the truth?" she snapped.

"I don't think you deserved any of this." I looked across

the room to find her eyes waiting to meet me in the middle. "And I'm sorry. I really am."

She didn't say anything. Not that I'd expected her to. But her body language spoke a thousand words; shoulders relaxed, facial expression eased. Even her gaze seemed to soften while we spent the next hour discussing the bizarre birthday party that my princess-tomboy little sister had talked me into. I honestly didn't know how or if I'd make things right with Deja. But I'd spend every ounce of energy necessary to give it all that I had.

CHAPTER FOUR

Orlando

It was Tuesday evening, probably my favorite day of the week. Since I'd moved back to Houston, I got to spend a lot more time with my baby sis. The twenty-five-year age difference didn't affect our bond at all. My mom hated the fact that I'd embraced her so easily, seeing as she was the product of an affair my father had.

From where I was sitting, their marital issues started years before Markie was even born. Moms was a control freak and Pops couldn't be controlled. It was a storm that had been brewing until finally it hit land.

"Lando, you shoulda seen how hard I hit him." My seven year old kid sister had been going on and on about how she was demonstrating hitting drills when she took out some kid during recess.

"I wrapped up just like you taught me to. And he was big. Like the size of a third grader!" Her hazel eyes lit up, sandy brown curls bouncing all over her head as she stretched her little arms wide and wrapped them around herself.

"Markayla, calm down so I can tackle your hair." Her mother, Darlene, reentered their living room from the back of the house. "She got another write up for these shenanigans you know." She cut her eyes at me.

Markie was the perfect blend of my father and her mother, with a freckled caramel complexion just like mine.

"If you'd let me put her in camp maybe she could burn off some of that energy," I suggested for the hundredth time, "She's an athlete, Darlene. It's in her blood."

"What's *in her blood* is torturing these poor kids who don't have access to the San Antonio Runners' two thousand nine first round draft pick." She shook her head, smoothing Markie's hair up into an afro puff on top of her head. "You need to stop encouraging this behavior. It's not like she'll ever be able to play in the league."

"Yes, I will!" Markie's little voice squeaked, popping up off the couch and planting her hands on her hips. "Lando said I can be whatever I wanna be and I wanna play for the San Antonio Runners!"

"Markie, go get your bag," Darlene fussed.

"But—"

"Now, Markayla Nicole," Darlene cut her off, pointing a long, light brown finger in the direction of Markie's room.

"Yes ma'am." The little woman marched off; bright orange sweatpants twisted at the waist because she'd challenged me to a wrestling match as soon as I walked through the door.

"You see that?" Darlene slanted her eyes toward Markie then brought them back to me. "All that attitude, that's your fault."

"Wait, what'd I—"

"She thinks she's a boy, Lando," she interrupted, "She wants to be just like you and she says it all the time. Can you tell her that there's a difference between the two of you? That she can't just go around performing hitting drills on little boys? They're gonna be bigger than her someday. And I don't need every mother in the neighborhood knocking at my door because their son's being physically abused by my little girl."

"Fine, I'll talk to her." I looked down at the petite woman who'd stolen my father's heart and held it for nine years.

Appearances might suggest that she wasn't more to him than looks, but Darlene's light skin, long curly hair, hazel eyes, and shapely figure paled in comparison to the mother she was to Markie and the wife she was to my pops. God only knew what a struggle it was to keep up with a man who lived a bulk of his life on the go. But she'd calmed him in so many ways. Even helped him invest all the money he'd made working in refineries for forty years, into something other than casinos, fast cars, and other women. And I'd never mention this to my mother, but it was Darlene who'd saved *Aroma*, the coffee shop Pops had opened for my mother as a wedding gift when I was just five years old. Pops was ready to pull the rug from under Mom's feet when their divorce got messy. But Darlene fought for her tooth and nail, mentioning something about weakening the waves of karma by standing in the gap for her husband's ex-wife. And of course, I stepped in and took over as soon as I was in a place to do so.

"Please." Her bright eyes widened. "I mean I know she's only seven, but she listens to you for some reason."

"Wow. It's almost like I'm her brother or something," I teased.

"Very funny," she returned, "And how's the party planning going? Miss Deja Blu still giving you a hard time?" She rested her narrow behind on the side of an armchair.

"Maaan," was all I could say. And Darlene laughed at my pain.

She shrugged. "I told you to save all that money and stress and throw the party right here at the house."

"But that ain't what Markie wants," I sighed.

Darlene rolled her eyes. "Because Markie's a spoiled brat."

"Okay, I'm ready." Markie halted our conversation, rushing back into the living room with her San Antonio Runners backpack and overnight bag in tow. "Are we still going to *Jump On It?*"

"Absolutely." I allowed her to grip my hand. "I heard they switched up the pizza."

"Oh, I hope it's better than last time." She rolled her eyes. "Mommy, can you believe they had the nerve to serve us fake cheese like we wouldn't notice?"

"Really?" Darlene said expressively, mouthing to me *"What?"* and I just shook my head.

"Sure did." Markie nodded. "It tasted like wax. We had to leave early and go to Sam's 'cause Sam's pizza has real cheese. And Lando bought a million rolls of toilet paper because he was starting a cleanse the next morning."

"You know what, let's get you outta here before you tell all my business."

"Okay?!" Darlene's face turned red from laughing. "I'll see you tomorrow after school, little woman." She leaned in and kissed Markie on the cheek.

"Ok Mommy. I love you." She blew a kiss as we headed toward the door.

"Love you, too. And thanks again, Lando. I appreciate you," Darlene said, rubbing a hand down my arm.

I smiled. "My pleasure. Tell Pops to hit me up when he gets in."

"Will do." And me and the little lady were on our way to *Jump On It*.

Deja

My feet hurt. Eyes hurt. Even my freaking scalp hurt. But I'd promised my baby a couple of hours of Mommy and DJ time before we headed home and a promise was a promise no matter how long the day had been. It wouldn't have been so bad if he was still a three-year-old and chose something simple like McDonald's or even the movies. But this seven-year-old had long outgrown the Play Land. He was ready to jump until the last second ran off the clock.

"Did you pack your grip socks like I told you?" I asked as we pulled into the parking lot of the new trampoline park, *Jump On It*, that had just opened a few miles from my parents' place.

"Yes ma'am. I got 'em right here."

I unbuckled my seatbelt and looked over my shoulder to find him pulling out a pair of blue socks with gripped padding on the bottom.

"Alright. Let's go." I grabbed my purse and climbed out, rounding the car to let him out of the backseat.

The place was fairly empty, seeing as it was Tuesday afternoon, so DJ would have most of the jumping space to himself. I spotted an empty lounge chair toward the back after paying for his admission and watched him kick out of his shoes and socks, to slip on what he called his JOIs.

"Baby, please, be careful," I warned as he headed up the steps to the first section of jumping space.

"I will!" he yelled back, running onto the mat, straight up to a little girl that I assumed he knew from school.

"Wow, are you stalking me?" A familiar voice sounded to my right. I looked up from checking notifications on my phone to find Orlando's broad shouldered ass standing there looking as beautiful as he always did.

"Didn't I leave you at the office?" I sighed, trying my best to be annoyed by his presence when deep down inside, I was starting to get used to it.

He nodded. "You did. Somebody sitting here?"

"Yes, my son," I lied for no reason.

"You mean the one over there jumping six feet in the air?" He smirked, full lips causing reactions in my belly that were extremely inappropriate for a woman who'd sworn she'd moved on.

"That would be him," I sighed, shoulders rising and falling as he took the seat beside me.

"Why don't I hold it for him?" The leather gave beneath his thick frame; his long legs spreading as he pulled his hands behind his head.

"So…" he spoke to break the awkward silence that settled between us and seemed so much louder in public.

"So…" I repeated because… hell, what else was I supposed to say?

"Things are looking pretty good for this party so far." Work. He brought up work. I guess that was a simple enough escape.

"Yeah, I agree." Why the hell did this have to be so awkward?

"What brings you to a trampoline park?" I asked, assuming he hadn't gone out and made any babies during our rift.

"My sister," he replied, "You know, the one you're helping me throw an extremely over-the-top party for?"

"Yeah. How could I forget?" I barely smiled, rolling my eyes when it didn't reflect how I was feeling inside at all.

"Are you thirsty? I'm pretty thirs—"

"Lando, come quick! Somebody got hurt!" The little girl that DJ had approached came running up on us, freckled face flushed red. And then it clicked that hers was the pretty face on all the invitations my team had created. It was scary how much she looked like Lando. The spitting freaking image.

Lando and I jumped up from our seats at the same time and rushed to the platform to find DJ sitting against the railing holding his stomach.

"DJ, are you okay?" I went down on one knee, grabbing both sides of his face and staring into his eyes.

"My stomach," he whined.

"What happened?" I panicked. He just shook his head and wouldn't answer me.

"DJ, you have to tell me what's wrong so I can take care of you. Did you fall or something?" I asked again.

"He didn't fall," Orlando's little sister spoke up, sparkling hazel eyes glossed with tears, "I hit him. I didn't mean to hurt him, though! I thought he was ready!"

"Markie!" Lando raised his voice. "What did we just talk about on the ride over?"

"I know. But he said he was ready!" Markie whined. "I'm sorry, DJ. Is he gonna die?" She looked up at me and melted my heart to pieces.

"No," I said, releasing one of DJ's cheeks to rub a hand down the side of her arm. "He's not gonna die, baby. He'll be alright. Okay?"

"Okay," she said, then looked over at Lando.

A moment later, a member of the staff came over to

check on us and I assured her that everything was fine before Lando went off to the side to speak with her.

Strange.

He was so attentive, even offered to drive us to the hospital. But I still wasn't with this newfound openness between us. I was getting closer, but I wasn't there.

*

"Mommy, when do we get to go home?"

DJ hated hospitals as much as I did. Mostly because all we ever got when we entered one was bad news. The first time he'd ever entered a hospital was to visit me after his father broke four of my ribs. And the second was when we first got to Houston and had to rush Mama to the emergency room. Both times I'd wished there'd been an alternative, but sometimes life happened before you got a chance to make plans. Hopefully, this visit would send him away on a lighter note. I only brought him in so I could sleep without all the what ifs in my head.

"DJ!" Markie's squeaky voice sounded at the hospital room door before I had the chance to answer DJ's question. Orlando insisted on following us over to make sure DJ was okay.

"I got you a get well bear from the gift shop," Markie said, "The cashier lady said I came just in time because some old man had his eye on this bear."

"Thank you, Markie. But I don't play with stuffed animals." DJ pushed the bear away and folded his arms across his chest, lying back in the bed and staring up at the ceiling.

"I'm sorry, baby," I apologized to Markie, "DJ's kind of in a bad mood because he doesn't like hospitals. How about I hold on to this until he gets home?"

She nodded and stepped away from the bed. "Okay. Is DJ mad at me?"

"I don't... he—"

"He wouldn't be if he knew what I know about that get well bear." Orlando stood at the threshold of the room, big frame occupying most of the doorway.

"What do you know?" DJ sat up straight, eyes wide with curiosity as he looked across the room at the big man by the door.

"Well, I don't know if yours has the same superpowers as the one I got when I was hurt," he said, walking into the room, "But I could check him out and let you know. I mean that's if it's okay with your mom."

"Mommy, give him the bear!" DJ almost yelled, swinging his feet over the side of the bed and pushing at my arm.

"Oh, ok. I guess," I said, playing along.

"Alright, let's see." Orlando took the bear from my hands, big palms reminding me how good it used to feel when he massaged my shoulders.

"Now the coloring looks good," he said, giving the medium sized bear a thorough examination, "Blue's always a good color for superpowers. It just makes sense, ya know?"

DJ nodded. "Uh huh. Blue's my favorite color. I knew there was a reason for that!"

I covered my mouth to hold in a chuckle as Orlando winked at me and continued.

"You know what else is important?" He stepped in closer to me and my son, so close that I could smell the enticing beard balm that filled up my office space every time he came in. "I mean aside from the ears, cause those are important for hearing get well wishes."

"What is it?" DJ swung his feet. "Please hurry. I need to know when I'm gonna get outta here!"

I chuckled again and Orlando and Markie almost did, too.

"It's the squeeze test," Orlando said, "If this bear can't pass the squeeze test, I'm afraid he might not be the right one."

"And how am I gonna know that? Are you gonna squeeze it?" DJ asked, eyes as wide as two saucers.

"Oh no." Orlando shook his head, extending the bear to DJ. "Only you can execute the squeeze test. It's your bear, not mine."

Orlando slanted his eyes to a smiling Markie. She'd apparently been through this routine before and it was the cutest thing I'd ever seen. DJ looked so serious, hesitantly taking the bear from Orlando's hand. And I swear, the clock on the wall stopped ticking as we waited for the squeeze test results.

"Well!?" Markie said, little shoulders raised, hands out to either side. "Did he pass the test or what?" She dropped a hand to her hip.

DJ's eyes went from me to Markie, then finally landed on Orlando when he said, "He passed!" with a mile-wide smile on his face. I hadn't seen him this happy since his first smash-cake.

Before any of us knew it, we were clapping our hands, having completely forgotten where we were in this tiny celebration. I hadn't laughed that long or smiled that hard in a long time, and it was gonna be impossible for me not to thank Orlando for what he'd done for my baby.

Orlando

"Alright, we're gonna head out. You and Mister DJ have school in the morning." I ruffled a hand through Markie's afro puff as we stood by DJ's bed after he'd received his discharge papers.

"Actually, can I...can I talk to you for a second outside?" Deja's request surprised me.

"Sure." I swept a hand toward the door before I slanted my eyes at Markie and DJ. "Stay put. No hitting drills." They both giggled.

"What's up?" I stepped out of the room to join a nervous looking Deja in the hallway.

"It's, I just...I wanted to thank you for...for what you did in there," she said, folding her arms across her chest.

"It's nothin'," I shrugged.

"It's more than nothing," she returned, "DJ has real bad hospital anxiety and you helped him out a lot. I don't think you know how much."

"Has he been in and out of the hospital a lot?" I squinted. DJ didn't look like a sickly kid. But kids are resilient. Sometimes you couldn't tell.

"No. No, nothing like that." She shook her head and raised a palm. "He's just seen a lot. In hospitals, I mean. It's a long story that I'd rather not share right now. But thank you. I just wanted to say thank you."

"What about later?" I couldn't pass on the opportunity. This was as close to open as she'd been.

"Huh?" she squeaked.

"The long story, I'd like to hear it. Maybe over dinner?"

"Lando—"

"I know, I know. It sounds like I'm asking you out on a date. But I swear, I'm not. I just like to hear stories."

"*Whatever!*" She smiled, pearly white teeth tugging at the core of my stupid emotions.

"Is that a whatever *yes* or a whatever *no?*" I asked. "And before you answer remember that you do owe me from saving your son's life." I raised both palms and shrugged my shoulders. It was a reach, but a necessary one at the time.

"You did no such thing, Mr. Theatrics." She was still smiling. That was a good sign.

"But you did offer comfort," she continued, unfolding her arms and stuffing her hands into the pockets of her skirt. "Yes."

"Yes, what?"

"*Lando.*"

"Alright, I'll chill."

"Good." She nodded. "And one more thing."

"Go ahead."

"When I offered the clerk my insurance card, she said the bill had already been taken care of. You know anything about that?" She looked up at me questioningly.

"Yeah," I replied, "It's company policy. He got hurt at *JOI.* so, *JOI* foots the bill."

"Oh, well… that makes sense. But what *doesn't* make sense is your name on a copy of DJ's billing papers right next to *JOI.*"

"Actually, that makes sense, too," I added, straightening in preparation to collect my little sister. "I'm the owner," I said, watching her face lift with surprise.

"I'll text you the details for our non-date. Dress comfortably. We might be jumping!"

She rolled her eyes then turned and walked back into the room, giving me the perfect view of that ample behind.

CHAPTER FIVE

Deja

A week had passed since the hitting drill at *Jump On It* and Orlando had sent a text asking about DJ every day. He was so consistent that his alert had become my alarm. And I appreciated that. And of course, DJ did too.

Things had been going surprisingly smooth between us. Something about the way he'd interacted with my son had softened me a bit. We weren't BFFs or anything like that, but now, when he brought me warm vanilla tea from the café, I no longer wanted to take the lid off and pour it in his lap.

The non-date that he'd bribed me into was tonight. I hadn't been out with male company in so long I had no idea what to wear. Luckily, my seasoned fashionista mother was home from the hospital and in good enough spirits to help. Even had enough pep in her step to pull out her old marcel curling iron set and do a little something with my hair.

"You know, I didn't think I'd like your hair like this, but it's cute. You've got the right head for it," she said, curling the shortest portion of my pixie cut and patting it the way she always did.

"Thank God I got your head and not Daddy's," I chuckled and so did she.

"Speaking of the Devil." She slid the iron into a slot on the thermal stove. "He's been around a lot lately. Did you throw a fit or something?" She parted another section of hair and pulled the curling iron out of its slot, swiftly curling my hair as if she could do it in her sleep.

"Kind of," I admitted, "Are you mad?"

"No," she replied abruptly, "Just surprised is all. I don't think I've woken up to the smell of eggs and bacon since you were DJ's age." She huffed out a chuckle, then breathed out a sigh.

"Deja, I need to tell you something," she started. I hated when she started sentences like that. It rarely led to anything good.

"Ma, not now. *Please*? It's been such a good day. You're feeling better. We got your meds under control. Can we just stay here for a minute? I'm begging!" I pled, knowing full well it wouldn't work.

"I love you, and you know that. You do know that, right?" She curved around my shoulder to catch my rolling eyes.

"Of course, I do," I replied on a sigh.

"Good. Then you should know that even if me and your daddy don't make it through this patch, it'll be okay. *We'll* be okay."

"Mama—"

"There's no need to go back and forth about it," she

cut me off, "You and I both know what your father's been up to all these years. And that doesn't just go away because I almost died. He's a man, Deja. And men have needs. Unfortunately, I can't fulfill them anymore."

"And why not?" I couldn't believe I was asking that question. And almost instantly I felt vomit rising in my throat at the thought of the potential response. "I mean not that it's any of my business, but you're a healthy, attractive woman. Am I missing something?"

"Actually, you are," she replied, "Deja, there's more to making love than just being attracted to somebody. And all those other things are what your father and I are lacking. I love James. Always have and always will. But too much has happened. Too much time has passed to repair what's been broken."

I didn't know what to say or if I was even supposed to say anything. I felt like the helpless little girl that had sat on the sofa and watched my daddy go in and out of front door like a visitor instead of the owner. I'd done all I could to try and pull them back together. Even took on all the chores on days when Mama was too stuck in her head to climb out of bed.

But it wasn't enough then and apparently wasn't enough now. All that wasted time on two adults who didn't see their marriage as something worth mending.

"Are you okay?" She walked around in front of me, grabbing both of my hands and pulling them up to her flat belly. "That's all that matters to me right now."

"I'm fine, Mama," I said, "just, can you gimme a minute? I need to go make a phone call."

"Oh no you won't." She dropped my hands and planted her palms on her hips. "You will *not* sit in this house and sulk over a failed marriage that wasn't yours to save. Especially not when the stars have finally aligned and brought my shoulda-been-son-in-law back in the picture."

She sucked her teeth, swinging her curvy hips as she hurried back behind me and resumed styling my hair.

"Tryna stiff my boy. Over my dead body!" she fussed, going to work on those curls. All I could do was smile. This woman was Orlando Terry's number one fan.

Orlando

"Which shirt says *I'm sorry my little sister sent your son to the hospital?*"

Markie'd hit me up on FaceTime to see if I was nervous about my non-date with Deja.

And I was.

Nervous as hell to be exact. Given our history, it would be easy for me to mess this up.

"The white one." Markie pointed at the screen while I held up two Polo shirts, one white and one red. "It makes you look innocent."

"That's racist," I whispered.

"No, it's not."

Damn, she heard me.

"The brain has a certain reaction to light that's different to its reaction to other colors. This is science, bro. And daddy told me I can't be racist because I'm Black."

I shook my head because there was no way I was going down that road with a seven-year-old who was apparently exploring options in other career fields just in case things didn't work out with the NFL.

"Alright, I'll take your word for it. You got anymore tips before I head out?"

She drummed her little fingers against her chin, the wall in her background adorned with a mix of Runners swag and tutus.

"Make sure you brush your teeth," she finally spoke, "We can't be sure that she's gonna kiss you, but you should be prepared just in case."

This kid...

"Thanks, Markie. Is that all?" I was afraid to ask.

"Oh yeah, did you condition your beard?" For some reason she always asked me that.

"You know I did!" I chuckled, rubbing a hand down the length of my beard. "Even used some beard balm."

"Good!" She smiled wide, looking up at the sound of her door creeping open. "Hey Daddy! Lando's got a date!" she greeted our Pops.

"Is that right?" I heard my father's voice then saw his face pop up on the screen as he sat down on Markie's bed. "Lookin' good, son."

"Like father, like son." I smiled at the sixty-five-year-old version of myself.

"You got that right!" He chuckled. "We gon' let you go. Call and give us an update, alright?"

"Will do. Love y'all," I said, blowing a kiss to the phone.

"Love you, too!" they both said in unison.

"How do you turn this off, baby girl?" Pops squinted, until Markie pressed the end call button and they vanished from the screen.

*

I'd told her to wear something comfortable but wasn't

prepared for how good she'd look in a pair of jeans and cropped sweater. Minimal makeup highlighted her brown skin and a pair of signature high heels influenced the sexiness in her step as she strode toward me at the center of the helipad on the property of my estate.

"You are so extra!" She smiled, her eyes roving over my shoulder to the helicopter I'd rented for the night.

"What? This old thing?" I glanced behind me then returned my eyes to a glowing Deja. "It's just for pictures. But we can take a ride if you want," I teased, brows hiked.

"Funny." She stepped forward, looking me up and down before she started her walk around the helicopter. "How do you know I'm not afraid of heights? This could've been a huge waste of money."

"If memory serves me right…" I turned around and headed in her direction after she'd completed her inspection. "You loved the thrill of being up in the air. Remember the Ferris wheel?"

"God, who could forget the Ferris wheel!?" She sighed, smiling wide as her eyes floated up to the night sky.

"Good times," I said, standing next to the helicopter, extending a hand and praying she'd take it.

"Yeah," she responded softly, taking the pilot's hand instead of mine. and climbing into her designated seat, following instructions to prepare for the flight.

"Where are we going?" she asked over the noise of the propeller after we'd secured our headsets.

"It's a surprise!" I shouted, looking down in response to her hand nervously gripping my thigh as we left the ground, the wind whirling beneath us parting the grass around the landing pad.

Deja

The city that nearly drove me to road rage on a daily basis looked like Christmas from two thousand feet in the air. Strings of red lights heading in one direction and white heading in the other. The landscape that seemed so cramped while we lived in it below seemed so spacious from up here and it was strangely fascinating.

I had no idea what Orlando had in store and I tried to be upset that he'd gone so overboard.

But it was hard.

Nearly impossible, if I was being honest. When he appealed to my fascination with living in the sky, how could I not like him just a little bit? Even my meanest parts were moved by that.

"You good over there?" he spoke into the mic connected to our headsets, taking notice of the easy smile that hadn't left my face.

"Yeah!" I pulled my eyes from the hypnotizing view below to look at him, butterflies waking up in my belly, sending my thoughts where they shouldn't go.

"Good. Put this on." He reached into the pockets of his jeans and pulled out a black scarf.

"What?" I wrinkled my nose.

"Don't worry, I'm not gonna push you out!" He grinned. "The destination is a surprise!"

"Lando—"

"I promise, it'll be worth it!" he insisted, "Here, turn around, I'll do it!" He loosened his safety belt and slid closer to me. I turned my back to him, feeling the heat from his body crowding my space, fighting the urge to react to his touch as he secured the scarf over my eyes.

"How many fingers am I holding up?" he asked, assisting me in sitting back in my seat, the scent of his crisp cologne sweeping past my nose.

"You know I could just lie, right!?" I smiled.

"Point taken!" I could hear the smile in his voice. "But you're not a liar!" I couldn't see his face when he said that, but I wished I could. I wanted to know if his expression matched the certainty in his voice.

"I can't see, Lando!" I honestly couldn't. "And I'm gonna kill you if my lashes are smooshed!"

"Your lashes are fine!" He assured me. "And if they're not, I got a spare set in my wallet!"

"My lashes ain't fake, negro!" I fussed, having no idea if his chest was close enough to poke.

And then he roped an arm around my shoulder, pulling me closer to his side as the helicopter descended, an action to which I did not object.

Orlando

Deja was nosy as hell, asking a million questions after we'd landed and climbed into my truck that a friend had brought out for me to drive the rest of the way since there wasn't enough landing space where we were going. It was only a fifteen-minute drive but she gave me hell the entire time. Which was exactly what I'd expected. She hadn't changed a bit.

"We're here." I pulled up in the parking lot of a place she'd surely remember once I uncovered her eyes.

"Sit tight. I'm coming to let you out." I tapped her

thigh then hopped out of the truck, hurrying around to the passenger side to open up her door.

"You got it?" I asked as she struggled with the seatbelt. "Lemme help you," I insisted, scared that she might break a nail.

The intoxicatingly soft scent swimming off her skin as I reached across her belly to unlatch the safety belt was almost enough to make my mouth water. I needed to get ahold of my damn self.

"Thank you." She didn't seem nervous or bothered by my touch, allowing me to take her hand and help her out of the truck. She took in a deep breath as her heels touched the pavement, lips curving with curiosity as she took in the sounds around us.

"Is that… do I smell funnel cake?" She gripped my hand tight, having no idea how much I'd missed her touch.

"I'on't know. You wanna take that scarf off?"

She nodded, cheekbones rising, long fingers clasped together in front of her as I stepped up behind her and untied the scarf.

"Heard you hadn't been here in a while," I said, sliding my hands from around her, watching as she came completely unglued, bringing a hand up to cover her mouth.

"The Carnival!" She took a step forward then remembered I was there and stopped to turn back and look at me.

"I didn't even know they still did this. This was our first…"

"I know."

"Why did you bring me here?" She looked up into my eyes. "What are we doing, Lando?" She dropped her hands to her sides, ripping the wind from my sails just when I thought we were getting somewhere.

"I'm sorry," I sighed, "If you wanna leave, if all this is too much, I understand."

"I don't." She surprised the shit out of me. "And it's not too much. It's…perfect, actually. At least it would've been if we'd brought the kids along. Listen, what are your intentions? Because you obviously put a lot of thought into this."

"I did," I chuckled, running a hand down my beard. "And I'm glad you noticed and didn't run off screaming or cursing me out. 'Cause honestly, that's what I expected."

"But you brought me here anyway?"

"Yeah."

"Why?" She asked a logical question; and luckily, I had a logical answer comprised of three simple words.

"I missed you." A simple truth I'd been carrying in hopes of sharing it with her someday.

"And I know I'm probably being too forward 'cause technically, this ain't supposed to be a date. But I can't help it, Dej. Sitting across from you pretending that I don't want you is the hardest thing I've ever have to do."

Silence was her response as she stared down at her shoes. "Say something. *Please*," I begged, needing her voice for validation, rejection, or whatever I was gonna get.

"Why now?" She raised her head slowly, expression laced with skepticism. "After all this time, after all this distance, why pour your heart out now?"

"I got to you as soon as I could," I replied, "You weren't having it any other way. You got married and had a son, Dej. Was I supposed to step up while you were married? Would you have respected that?"

"Of course not." Her eyes crinkled. "But there was time before that. You coulda made this right a long time ago. Now we're just…"

"Just what, thirty-two apiece?" I mentioned. "If age is

your excuse, you gotta come better than that. We got plenty of time if this is what you want."

"But what if it's not?"

God, I didn't see that coming. Was she really about to kill what little hope I thought I had?

I took a deep breath, never taking my eyes away from her. The moonlight kissed her cheek at the perfect angle and I knew I wasn't making a mistake.

"I never considered that," I replied. Had I thought too long on being rejected, this whole night may never have happened.

"Well you should have," she said, folding her arms across her chest, "Do you know how arrogant this is? How egotistical and self-centered you have to be to think that I'd be impressed by an old helicopter and a carnival that should've been shut down decades ago? I'm not that same little college girl who was blown away by your theatrics, Lando. I'm a grown woman. There's more to me than that."

"I know that."

"No, you don't. You don't know that because you don't know *me*."

That was it. It wasn't gonna happen. I'd done what I thought was best and it still wasn't enough. Pops was right when he told me that breaking a woman's heart was the only mistake you could never fully recover from. I needed to come to grips with the fact that for me, Deja Blu Huffington would forever be the one who got away.

"Ok." I nodded glancing down at my feet. "I can... I can take you back to your car." I slid my eyes up to find her almost smiling.

"Is that what you got from what I just said?" she asked, stepping in closer to me.

"Yeah, I mean it's... that's what you want, right?"

"No," she replied, "it's not." She reached out for my hand and of course, I accepted.

"Don't get me wrong, I'm flattered by all of this." She gripped my hand. "But you do *not* wanna see what happens on the roundabout if I eat even a bite of that funnel cake." She chuckled. The sweetest sound in the world.

I blew out a sigh of relief , finally feeling a sense of familiarity with the closeness of our bodies. "So, what do you wanna do?"

She smacked her lips. "You coulda saved a lotta money by asking me that in the first place. Pizza. Takeout. At your place because my current residence is full of old people sorting through divorce proceedings."

"You sure?" I asked, because with Deja I had to.

"As sure as I have ever been." She hooked an arm through mine, staring up at me in a way that she hadn't in a long time.

CHAPTER SIX

Orlando

"You think she liked it?"

I was pretty sure that wasn't a valid question seeing as every kid in attendance at *Markie's Touchdown Tutu Birthday Bash* was passed out under custom tents in the endzone at Runner Stadium.

"*Liked?*" My eyes went wide, cutting toward the fifteen little people who were wasted on fun and birthday cake. "They literally played until they passed out. I'd say this one was a win."

Deja chuckled, taking a deep breath of victory as I hooked an arm through hers and took a stroll along the fifty yard line, still blown away at just how many pink, red, and gold balloons and confetti were still covering the bright green turf.

"I think Markie's exact words were, *Lando, this is astro-*

nomical!" I threw my hand up to mimic my sister's enthusiasm and Deja busted out laughing.

She and her team had gone above and beyond my wildest expectations. From Markie and her friends running out onto the field with the actual San Antonio Runners, red smoke and all. To the Misty Copeland appearance that had Markie believing she could do football and ballet too. To the crazy Iron Man obstacle course that had my old ass racing against kids with new knees. To the larger than life Super Bowl finale where Markie got to invite her friends on an all-expense paid weekend trip to Disney World, taking place the very next day. All of it was right up Markie's alley and she'd be thanking me for years for making up with Deja. The woman might not have known it, but my baby sis would make it clear as soon as she woke up. She was now amongst Markie's top five favorite people, along with me, her parents, and Beyoncé.

"She is somethin' else." Deja laughed. "And so are you." She looked up into my eyes, giving no fuss as I pulled her in against my side and planted a kiss on her soft lips.

"Am I?" I stopped our stride to turn and face each other.

"Yes, you are." A smile parted her lips. "The only person smiling harder than Markie today was you. And I think that's beautiful. I think *you're* beautiful."

I tried to act hard, like being called *beautiful* didn't affect me. But when Deja said it, when Deja said anything to me at all, it took on new meaning. We'd only been at this reconnecting thing for two months, but it felt like longer with the way she was opening up. She wasn't hesitating or holding back, almost like the old Deja but more articulate. Aside from the pain I'd caused, I was kind of happy that we'd parted ways. That separation had given us both a chance to grow into who we needed to be for each other. It was funny how things had come full circle. How we'd finally been restored.

"And you're beautiful, too." I leaned in and pecked her lips, squeezing my arms tight around her waist, silently promising myself that I would never let her go again.

Deja

After three torturous months of living with my dysfunctional parents, I'd finally decided that I needed my own place. I told myself that it wouldn't be permanent because I'd outgrown the familiarity of Houston. But DJ loved everything about it because some of his favorite people were here. I'd admit that living this close to Desmond was a good thing for our son. He got to spend as much time as he wanted with him, no longer having to take that forty-five-minute plane ride that always made my nerves bad. I did, however, have to set some boundaries for my ex. For whatever reason, he'd assumed that me having my own place meant that he could stop by unannounced. But that was quickly thrown out the window when I put him in his place. And by *place* I meant far away from my love life, since Orlando had been putting his best foot forward in securing that spot.

"Where you want this?" A now, constant fixture in my life, emerged from down the hallway holding an unmarked box that I didn't remember packing.

"I have no idea what that is. Just put it in the dining room." I stood up on my tiptoes and looked across the kitchen bar.

"*Or* you could open it and tell me where to put it now," he insisted, walking his fine ass into my kitchen wearing a pair of joggers that made my mouth water, crowding all my space, roping his arms around me and placing the box on the counter in front of me.

"I do not have time to be unboxing anonymous junk, Lando" I fussed, glaring at him over my shoulder. "I got a whole apartment to unpack, baby. I'll check it out later." I leaned back and kissed his cheek.

"What about if I say please?" He kissed my neck and backed up to lean against the countertop behind him. "I'm just tryna help. I mean I was taking care of the bedroom and this was just sitting there."

"Oh it was, was it?" I smirked.

"Yeah. Just, a big ass box in the middle of the bed. *Weird*."

"Yeah, just like you." I rolled my eyes and turned back to the box.

It only took a second to get the tape off the top, and inside the big box was a smaller box. This went on for a series of four boxes, and I was about to roll my eyes out of socket when I finally made it to the last one and turned around to find Orlando down on one knee.

"You—"

"Don't curse!" He cut me off and grabbed ahold of my hand. "I know we haven't talked about this and you probably wanna be settled and all that. But I just wanna state my intentions, so we're not confused about where this is going."

He reached into his pocket and pulled out the ring that I thought was in the ring box behind me. Not allowing me to catch my breath, he pulled my hand to his lips and kissed it, warming me from the tips of my toes to the highest curl on my head.

"Deja Blu, I love you," he said, "I always have and I always will. I never thought I'd get to tell you that again. And now that I have, I wanna say it every day for the rest of my life. So..." He held out a sparkling, princess cut diamond ring that I definitely would have picked out if he'd lined it up next to ten others. "Will you marry me?"

"Yes!" I could barely breathe but didn't need to for that response. "Yes, Orlando, I'll marry you!"

He slipped the ring onto my shaking finger and stood from the floor, roping his arms around my waist and swallowing me up into a dizzying kiss. My feet left the ground, swept up by his embrace. Lando felt so good against me I couldn't help but to cry.

"I love you so much." I pecked his lips and pulled back to stare into his eyes. "Is this real?" I asked, admiring the rock on my finger.

"What, the ring? Hell yeah!" His deep voice hiked.

"No, *this*! *Us*!" I smiled, body tingling with excitement.

"Does it feel real?" He sat me on top of the counter, pushing my legs farther apart and stepping in tight between them.

I pulled my bottom lip between my teeth and braced my palms on the counter on either side of my thighs.

"I don't know. Lemme see it," I whispered, eyes traveling down to the bulge growing beneath his pants.

"You sure? We ain't married yet," he teased, tracing his tongue across those sexy pink lips.

"That didn't stop us last night or the night before that," I reminded him, tugging at his waistband, my mouth watering at the thought of what I knew lie beneath.

"You got a point." He grinned as he pushed his pants down to his knees, rolled my sundress up to the top of my thighs, and swept my panties aside with his finger.

"Ooh," I moaned in response to his fingers slipping

inside me, nipples pressing into his chest as my back arched forward.

"You're so wet." He leaned in and kissed my neck, my heart pounding against my breasts as he stroked me nice and slow.

"Is that for me?" He asked a question he already knew the answer to. I'd been his from the beginning, no matter how long it took to get me back.

"Yes," I purred, rolling against his palm. "It's all yours." My ass slid against the cool counter, tight with desperate need to be opened even wider.

After using a free hand to reach down and grab a condom from his pocket, Orlando sheeted himself and pulled me to the edge of the counter. Kicking out of his pants, he pushed his flesh against my opening, shoving into me deep, sending flashes of light before my eyes.

"Shit, Deja!" he mumbled, pumping into me hard, hands tight around my waist.

"You love this pussy, don't you? Say you love it!" I commanded. The thought of such a big man being power-less to my warmth turned me on in ways that he couldn't possibly understand.

"I love it." He sucked his teeth, straightening his back to stare into my eyes. "This is mine, you hear me? For fuckin' ever!" He slammed into me forcefully, pushing my legs open wider so he could burrow into me deeper and make good on his word.

I ripped my dress over my head, too hot to be wearing anything but lust and admiration for the beautiful man standing before me. My heart thumped in my chest like the baseline to my favorite song. My lips parted with the desire to be taken into his. Orlando's hands gripped my thighs as he stared down at me possessively, sucking my nipples hard and long then laving his tongue over them to soothe the sting, hungrily taking me stroke by stroke to the only place I wanted to be.

"Do you hear me, Deja Blu?" he asked again, strumming my swollen and exposed clit with the pad of his thumb, golden abs glistening with sweat, face contorting as he neared climax.

"Yes." I shivered, warmth pooling in my belly. "I hear you, baby. Fuck!" He thrust into me deeper, filling me to capacity as his thighs began to tense.

Panting and moaning nearly inaudible obscenities about how tight my pussy was and how he was about to bust, he pulled me down from the counter and flipped me over onto my stomach, laying me bare and exposed for him to do what he pleased.

"Shit, Lando!" I couldn't hold it in as he pushed a knee between my legs and swept them apart, shoving into me from behind.

My breasts jolted forward from being fucked so hard, tight nipples pressed against the cold edge of the countertop. I begged him to fuck me harder with his hands gripping my hair. His big body pressed against the back of me as he leaned in to suck the sensitive skin on my neck before bathing it with his tongue to pacify the sting.

"Can I cum in this pussy?" he moaned in my ear, hungrily sucking my earlobe, wet noises from his mouth driving me insane.

"Cum in me, baby." I granted full permission, dull pains prickling my walls as he forced my body to conform to his girth.

I threw it back at him as hard as I could, full to capacity with fire and desperation, on the brink of succumbing to a climax of my own. The walls closed around us and white noise rang in my ears as Lando shoved into me and tightened his hold around my waist, stroking me with precision until I shivered in his embrace, only then surrendering to his own inevitable undoing.

He collapsed against my back, still submerged inside me, soothing my throbbing walls.

"You wanna finish unpacking?"

"Fuck them boxes," I happily replied, squealing as he stood up, rolled me over and lifted me up, wrapping my legs around his waist and hurrying me off to the bedroom.

THE END

ABOUT SABRINA B. SCALES

Sabrina B. Scales is a national best-selling author of vibrant and passionate romance whose unique style of writing highlights real stories about real people falling in real love.

Text **BRICKIE** to 66866 for exclusive updates!

For more information, please visit her website at www.sabrinabscales.com

 facebook.com/AuthorSabrinaBScales

 twitter.com/SabrinaBScales

 instagram.com/authorsabrinabscales

ALSO BY SABRINA B. SCALES

Naughty

Nasty

Plus

COMING SOON FROM ROSE GOLD
PRESS

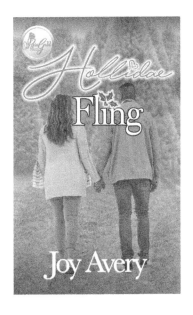

Hollidae Fling

by Joy Avery

Made in the USA
Monee, IL
07 February 2021

59731280R00125